THE KILLING BREED

THE KILLING BREED

FRANK LESLIE

WHEELER PUBLISHING
A part of Gale, Cengage Learning

GALE
CENGAGE Learning™

Detroit • New York • San Francisco • New Haven, Conn • Waterville, Maine • London

GALE
CENGAGE Learning

LIBRARY OF CONGRESS CATALOGING-IN-PUBLICATION DATA

Leslie, Frank, 1963–
    The killing breed / by Frank Leslie. — Large print ed.
       p. cm. — (Wheeler Publishing large print western)
    Originally published: New York: Signet, 2008.
    ISBN-13: 978-1-59722-904-3 (pbk. : alk. paper)
    ISBN-10: 1-59722-904-0 (pbk. : alk. paper)
    1. Large type books. I. Title.
    PS3552.R3236K55 2009
    813'.54—dc22   2008045496

Published in 2009 by arrangement with NAL Signet, a member of Penguin Group (USA) Inc.

*For Bob King,
teacher and friend*

CHAPTER 1

The gnarled, bony hand grabbed the bottle around its neck and raised it to the dying light slanting through the dusty, west-facing window. The hand tipped the bottle back, and the man raised his head — an unshaven death's-head of pale, gaunt, drunken misery — from the pillow.

About three inches of whiskey remained. Good.

Neither he nor the girl would have to go downstairs for more. Not for another hour or two, anyway. It was too cold for the man to go, and he didn't want the girl to go and take with her the warmth of her young, supple body. Hours ago, he'd let the fire in the main saloon hall die. Too much work to split wood and haul it in from outside to feed the flames that, like the flame inside the man, seemed to be eternally dying.

"Got enough?" the girl asked, curled up against him, running a slender brown finger through the coarse gray hair on his chest.

She luxuriated in the feather mattress and the sheets that had been shipped from Denver when the saloon was still making money, and when there were more girls than only her, Ruby, a half-breed orphan from Montana Territory. She'd come from mining camps in Montana and Dakota where she'd plied her trade in drafty plank shacks with little more than straw pallets to work and sleep on, making so little that when she'd come here riding a stolen mule to the gold camps farther up the mountains, she hadn't weighed a hundred pounds.

Bill Thornton nodded and lifted the bottle to his lips, his eyes rolling back at the soothing fire of the whiskey that plunged down his throat and into his belly.

Ruby smiled and lifted her head slightly, her coffee brown eyes peering into his. She slid her hand down his chest and belly, found him beneath the quilts, and gently squeezed. "Again?"

Anything to please him, so he'd have no thoughts against keeping her here in this run-down saloon on an abandoned freight trail on the eastern slopes of the Colorado Rockies. Here, where he'd get maybe thirty customers a month. He used to get more than that in a single weeknight, when the trail outside the saloon was still a main thoroughfare for miners, freighters, drummers, and stagecoaches. Then he'd easily make a hundred dollars on the whores alone, three or four times that on hooch and his deftly weighted roulette wheel.

Thornton chuckled and set the bottle beside him, running his free hand through the long black hair falling down the girl's curving back. "You flatter me. I'm lucky to get it up once a week."

For some reason, she found this funny, chuckling as she rested her head once more on the pillow, showing the gap where she'd lost an eyetooth. Thornton wasn't offended. She wasn't mocking him. Ruby was a little touched, and who wouldn't be after the life she'd had? Besides, she took care of him, tending the saloon when his side ached too much for him to do anything but lie in bed or sit downstairs by the fire and kill the near-constant pain of the unhealed wound with rye.

Killing the pain and the memory of the girl who'd shot him. *Trying* to kill it, rather. Enough whiskey would soothe the raw ache in his side — a festering, stinging burn that he often imagined to be that of a rat trying to chew its way out from inside him. But it never took away the image of the girl who'd given it to him.

Faith . . .

The memory of the derringer slug drilling his side made him wince as though he'd been slapped — the wound had nearly healed once, then reopened when he'd taken a drunken fall. It had formed a couple of thin scabs but had never fully healed. Now it looked like raw meat greened by too much time in the sun, and it wept a thick yellow puss liberally laced with blood.

Thornton sucked a sharp breath against the old rage kindling inside him again. Beside him, the girl dozed, snoring softly, and he raised the bottle once more, blinking away the image of the blonde he'd once employed here — the beguiling Faith with her frank blue eyes, husky laugh, hourglass figure with firm, ripe breasts, a heart-shaped mole on her neck, and another nearly the same shape under her right breast.

She had a near-perfect body, but it was more than her body, Thornton knew, that had made her the main attraction of his roadhouse for nearly two years, and which had made him a wealthy and respected man. It was her earthy charm and wit as well as an aloofness that, although she gave her body, kept her spirit her own — inviolate, mysterious, and singularly alluring.

There was something about that elusive spirit that made men want to tame it. Thornton himself had wanted to; in fact, he'd thought he had. The chewing burn in his side reminded him that he hadn't come close. . . .

After she'd shot him and taken off with the half-breed who'd done odd jobs about the place — Yakima Henry — Thornton's luck had soured. For that reason, sometimes consciously, sometimes unconsciously, he blamed her for *all* of it — his ruined health *and* his ruined business.

Ruby lifted her head suddenly from the pillow, frowning. Her ears were better than Thornton's, and it was several seconds later that the roadhouse proprietor heard the drum of hooves outside, and then the squawk of tack and the rattle of bridle chains. Male voices rose as the hoof clomps grew.

"We have business!" Ruby trilled, rising to a sitting position, letting the quilts fall to reveal her large, swaying brown breasts as she turned toward the window.

She started to climb over Thornton toward the floor, but he gently pushed her back. "Hold on, girl."

Cursing, he dropped his pale, thin legs to the floor and rose, wincing at the hitch in his side. He grabbed the top quilt off the bed and, wrapping it around his shoulders while holding the whiskey jug in one hand, shuffled to the window.

He rarely got any business during the week; most of it came on Friday and Saturday nights, and even that was mostly from the same four or five men working diggings along the nearby creeks, and from a couple of Swedes raising horses over in Bobcat Valley. Few men but the occasional grub-line rider or desperado on the lam rode the trail during the week.

Thornton looked out into the yard where dust and leaves swirled in the raw late-September wind. Four riders had pulled up in front of the roadhouse. They sat their horses abreast, curiously looking around. Because there were a couple of broken windows, the porch boards were rotted with weeds pushing up from beneath, and there was no smoke rising from the fieldstone chimney, they no doubt wondered if Thornton was open.

Thornton himself often wondered. *Was* he open? What was the point in running the place with as little business as he got? But then, it no longer had any market value, and while he'd managed to save a sizeable nest egg, he had nowhere else to go even if his health would allow him to travel.

"Go away," Thornton grumbled, appraising the men sitting their horses below — five hard-looking, unshaven hombres in heavy fur coats, with rifles in oiled saddle scabbards, revolvers and knives jutting from sheaths on their hips or thighs. The long black hair of one of the riders — the man with the black stovepipe hat banded with snakeskin — swirled around in the wind. The angling late-afternoon light touched a small tattoo forming a green-blue cross on his forehead, just above the bridge of his nose.

Lowry Temple. Shit. He was ramrod of the bunch gathered around him now — three other American regulators and a Mexican pistolero named Chulo Garza.

"Go away," Thornton grumbled again, setting the bottle on the dresser to his left and reaching for the .38 revolver hanging by its butt ring from a wall hook.

Temple lifted his head to shout above the moaning wind, "Thornton, you in there?"

Thornton let his hand freeze on the pistol's butt and squinted down into the yard, studying the face of the man who'd yelled. It was Temple, all right. He dropped his hand from the .38 and, grunting his disgust at having to traipse downstairs,

13

tossed the robe onto the bed and reached for his balbriggans.

"Friends?" the girl asked.

"Friends?" Thornton chuckled. "Lowry Temple is no friend. Let's just call him an ex-employee. Bastard still owes me for a man he didn't kill."

When he'd stepped into his threadbare longhandles and donned heavy wool socks, he grabbed his tattered robe off a wall hook, then reached for the quilt. "Did a couple of small jobs for me three years ago and still thinks *I* owe *him* free hooch and a bed whenever he pulls through."

"Thornton!" Temple called once more.

"I'm comin'!" the roadhouse proprietor shouted at the window.

He dropped the .38 into one robe pocket, the bottle into another, stepped into wool-lined elk-skin slippers, and opened the door with another shrill curse. "Stay here, Ruby," he said as he stepped into the hall and began drawing the door closed behind him. "Don't want these wolves befouling you, girl. That younker that rides with Temple — Benny Freeze — carries clap like a polecat carries rabies."

Thornton shuffled downstairs in his slippers and shivered as the chill of the cavernous main saloon hall, with its long, scarred

14

bar and twenty or so tables, pushed against him.

As he descended the stairs, he ran a hand down the rail, his palms scraping several of the jagged holes that had been torn from the wood the night the half-breed had shot his way out of there, hopscotching tables while most of the men in the saloon had triggered lead at him. Earlier that night, the breed, Yakima Henry, had carved up four men who had tried to disfigure Faith to settle an old score with Thornton.

Those dead men had had friends and relatives downstairs that night, and the others took umbrage with *any* breed who killed a white man for *whatever* reason.

Thornton didn't mind that Henry had saved Faith. What he did mind was that the breed had been diddling the whore for free and that, the next day, she'd run off with him like a love-struck schoolgirl.

Yakima Henry had moved like a phantom, dodging bullets, swinging from chandeliers, and finally flying through the big plate-glass window at the room's front as though he'd suddenly sprouted wings.

He'd disappeared into the night, stealing back to the roadhouse the next day to retrieve the girl Thornton had thought was his own.

Faith.

Before she'd left, however, she'd given the roadhouse proprietor something to remember her by. Thornton had been about to punish her for sleeping with the breed behind his back with the traditional knife slash across the lips — which she had richly deserved despite her insistence that she and the half-breed were only friends — when she'd pulled the pearl-gripped derringer from some hidden sheath in her underclothes.

Unconsciously, Thornton brushed his hand against his perpetually blazing side — a doctor in Denver told him the surgery required to clean out the infected tissue in and around his ribs would, in his frail state, likely kill him — and began clomping across the main saloon hall. The big, bullet-shaped stove in the middle of the room had long since gone cold, and the only light in the place was the wan gray shafts pushing through the dirty, fly-specked windows and around the planks nailed over the broken ones. Thornton removed the locking bar from over the two outside doors, tossed it onto the floor with an echoing bang, and pulled one of the doors open with a raucous rake of rusty hinges.

The five riders had tied their horses to the

hitch rail and were mounting the boardwalk, the wind rippling the fur on their coats, boots thumping and spurs chinking. Lowery Temple had an incredulous look on his hawkish, mud-eyed face as he cast his glance across the saloon's front wall and then to Thornton, giving the roadhouse proprietor a bemused up-and-down.

"Didn't know the Comanche were raidin' this far north."

"Goddamnit," Thornton growled. "If I'm open, I'll have the sign saying as much in the front window. Now, if you'll excuse me . . ."

But before he could reach back to close the door, the tall, broad-shouldered Temple stepped forward, removing his stovepipe hat and swiping it across his legs to dislodge the trail dust. His voice even, his eyes hard, he growled, "Thanks for invitin' us cold, trail-weary pilgrims into your more-than-humble abode, Thornton. Why, you must be a real God-fearin' man to be so hospitable." The bounty hunter turned to Thornton, a sneer making his iron gray eyes sparkle.

Thornton stepped back with a sigh as the other four riders followed Temple into the room, a cold draft dogging their heels and blowing leaves over the threshold. The stocky, fiery-eyed blond, Frank Miller, gave his hat brim a wry pinch, while the young clap carrier, Benny Freeze, chuckled sneeringly, the tip of his tongue jutting out from between his little teeth.

The Mexican, Chulo Garza, stared blankly at Thornton as he pushed on past him, while Kooch Manley, stocky, paunchy, fat faced below his weather-stained Stetson, clapped his gloved hands and said, "I been wantin' a drink for the last five miles!"

Scowling, Thornton closed the door. He kicked at the dancing leaves, then turned to the five bounty hunters standing with their backs to him, appraising the grim environs. He grumbled, "Don't expect much. I'm out of beer, low on whiskey, and my girls have all drifted to rosier meadows."

Lowry Temple stood facing the room between Garza and Freeze, turning his head slowly and whistling softly. "What the hell happened, Thornton? I know it's a weeknight an' all, but Christ!"

Thornton cursed as he shuffled toward the bar. "Didn't you hear? The mine company in Gold Cache moved the main trail five miles south. What brings you out to this backside of the devil's hell? Lost, are you?"

"Me and the boys had business nearby," Temple said. The other men were sauntering over to a table near the stove, pulling off their gloves and looking around with grim bemusement. "Bobcat Canyon, matter of fact."

Thornton fished a bottle of cheap rye whiskey off a sparsely populated shelf beneath the bar, and frowned at Temple, who still stood in front of the door. "Bobcat Canyon? That's where the Johanssen brothers ranch."

Temple smiled devilishly as he bit the end off a long black cheroot. "Not anymore they don't."

Near the stove, fiery-eyed Frank Miller threw his head back and laughed.

CHAPTER 2

"Christ," Thornton muttered, carrying the bottle of rye and five shot glasses out from behind the bar, his elk-skin slippers sweeping the worn puncheons. "Oscar and Knute Johanssen were two of my few remaining regulars. And they made damn good gooseberry wine."

"Nice fellas, too." Frank Miller tossed his tan hat onto the table, around which he and the others except Temple sat, and ran a hand through his close-cropped blond hair. His crazy blue eyes seemed lit from a conflagration inside his head, and his bull neck was sunset pink. "They cooked us a nice supper, let us sleep in their barn. Even served us breakfast. If they'd had a daughter, I don't doubt they would have passed her around!"

He and the others laughed.

Thornton shook his head as he set the glasses on the table. "And you repaid their hospitality by killing them."

"A neighbor wanted 'em out," Temple said with a shrug.

Thornton sighed. "You're a strange breed."

The bounty hunter chuckled as he moseyed up to the table, stretching from side to side to loosen his back. "Am I mistaken, or was that you who hired me to kill three of your competitors up the canyon only — what was it? — two years ago?"

"They were conniving sons o' bitches." Thornton was filling the shot glasses. "Had no business in *my* canyon. Bastards and swine crowdin' my territory. I'd hire you to kill 'em all over again!"

He raised the bottle and turned to Temple, who now stood behind Benny Freeze. "But if you remember, that cheating cardsharp, Wendell Myers, is running with his tail up and his tongue flapping between Bismarck and Deadwood. I paid you to bring me his ears!"

" 'Do not judge, lest ye be judged,' " Temple clucked as he sank into a chair and ran his hand over a bullet hole in the table before him. "Mine company come in and shoot up the place, too?"

"Might as well have." Thornton raised the bottle to his lips and took a long pull.

21

Lowering the bottle, he stared down at the table, around which the bounty hunters sat, drinking and smoking. "Moving that trail was like cutting my head off slow with a rusty saw."

The old, familiar rage set the wound aflame once more, as though the whore were drilling him all over again with that pearl-gripped derringer. The girl, the half-breed, and the mining company's new road were a single, jeering enemy, constantly prodding his festering wound — laughing, heckling, applauding the hopeless abyss into which his life had plunged.

"I'd hire you to pluck the eyes from the skull of the son of a bitch that made *that* fine decision, only I'd probably have to send you to New York or Philadelphia to do it." Thornton slammed the bottle onto the table and held out his hand. "That'll be five dollars, and I'm in the unfortunate position of no longer being able to extend credit . . . even to my friends."

"Five dollars?" grunted the Mexican, Garza, who wore his black hair in several thin braids wrapped in greased rawhide. He extended his hand toward his half-empty shot glass. "For this javelina juice?"

"You know how much it costs to have supplies hauled up here to this pimple on the devil's backside?"

"I'll take it out of what you still owe me for the previous job I done for you." Temple scowled across the table at the roadhouse proprietor and threw back his entire shot, gritting his teeth as though he'd just eaten a lemon, rind and all. "You sent me to kill three men and a woman. I had to kill a coupla whores, too, and you didn't pay me for that."

"You didn't have to kill the whores. You just *like* killin' whores."

"They mighta sent me down the river."

"You're cloudin' the issue. I'm talkin' about that sharpie, Wendell Myers."

"Temple don't like the temptation of whores," said the middle-aged gent, Kooch Manley, laughing as he puffed on his stogie. "On account of his ma bein' . . ."

Apparently thinking twice about finishing his sentence, Manley let it trail off, flushing slightly as he scowled into the cigar smoke webbing around his head.

"A what?" Temple said, keeping his voice low and even. "A *whore?* That's right, Kooch — she was a whore. Only my mama was a God-fearin' whore." He leaned forward suddenly, jutting his head toward Manley, who sat across the table from him. He tapped his forehead. "That's who done gave me this here tattoo, don't ya know!"

A heavy silence filled the room, thick as tar. The men looked around at one another skeptically, bracing themselves as though they expected Temple to suddenly fill his hands with iron and start shooting. The walls creaked as the wind moaned. A loose outbuilding door thumped against its frame.

"Christ!" Thornton snapped his still-outstretched hand closed as he turned toward the stove. "Your misguided sense of entitlement is worse than Bardoul's, Temple."

"Bardoul?" said Frank Miller, raising his pale brows. "You know Wit Bardoul?"

"*Knew* him," Thornton corrected as he opened the stove door and set a pile of pinecones and feather sticks onto the cold ashes within. "Been pushin' up daisies since fall before last, up around Sundance Gulch. He was foggin' the trail of one of my whores and a wild-assed half-breed. Near as I can figure, the half-breed gave him a pill he couldn't digest."

"And vamoosed with the whore?" said Manley, chuckling.

"You got it." Thornton struck a match and set it under the tinder inside the stove. "Haven't seen hide nor hair of 'em since."

"Damn," Temple said, holding his shot glass up to his eye like a spyglass. "You're

24

getting too relaxed in your old age, Thornton. A breed running off with one of your whores? Can't imagine you standin' for that."

"I didn't stand for it. That's why I sent Bardoul."

"And Bardoul's dead." Frank Miller wagged his head, his crazy eyes still bright but somehow forlorn. "Imagine that. Wit Bardoul . . . *dead*."

Frank Miller laughed as he poured another drink. "That's a sad story."

"Yeah, it's sad, all right," said Manley. He looked at Thornton. "Why don't you bring us another bottle of that panther juice so we can drown our sorrows over the loss of a fellow bounty hunter — a god amongst men?"

"Yeah, another bottle," Benny Freeze said.

Thornton shoved a couple of small branches onto the fledgling flames, then closed the stove door and began pushing off his knee. The movement aggravated the festering wound in his side, and he grimaced, gaining his feet and scuffing toward the bar. "Why not? No others around to drink with."

"Wit Bardoul — dead." Frank Miller shook his head, sending thick puffs of cigarette smoke toward the bullet-riddled

25

wagon wheel chandelier not quite centered above the table. "That's hard to believe. I worked with Wit a time or two. Taught me a few things about trackin' and shootin'."

Temple poured out another round of drinks, finishing the first bottle. "Bardoul was a bushwackin', whoremongerin' fool."

Frank Miller glanced at his leader, his blue eyes fairly glowing with contempt, and for several stretched seconds it looked as though he might voice umbrage with Temple's estimation of Miller's deceased mentor. Apparently deciding against it, he muttered a curse, lifted his shot glass, and downed the whiskey in a gulp.

Returning from the bar, Thornton set another bottle of inferior rye on the table. He hauled his own bottle out of his robe while angling a chair toward the cracking stove whose heat was beginning to nibble at the room's dense chill.

"Who'd you say it was took him down?" Miller asked him.

Thornton took another pull from his bottle, set it on his thigh, and turned to Miller. He enunciated his words carefully as he stared at the stove. "Henry. Yakima Henry. Green-eyed half-breed. Shot up my place. Ran off with my best whore. Killed every man I sent after him."

Thornton turned to sweep his gaze across the bounty hunters lounging around the table to his left. They stared back at him through the room's gloom and webbing wood and tobacco smoke.

Thornton's heart quickened slightly. He licked his lips, felt an eager smile twitch at his mouth. "I don't know . . . you boys *might* be able to take him down . . . if you all went after him. Long odds, still."

"Like I said," Temple growled, leaning back in his chair. "Bardoul was a fool. Harvested bounties by shootin' men in the back. Wouldn't take much of a man to snuff his wretched wick." He cast a challenging glance toward Miller, whose jaws hardened in anger. "Bound to happen sooner or later."

"Oh?" Thornton cocked an eyebrow at the tattooed gent. "This half-breed isn't any normal man. You should've seen him dancing across the tables right here in this very room, dodging bullets triggered at him from every direction. Then he swung from that chandelier over there and crashed through the window . . . *gone!*"

Thornton pretended to study each of the bounty hunters, coldly critical. Then he pursed his lips, shook his head, and turned back to the stove. "Nah," he muttered, raising the bottle to his lips. "Forget it."

"Forget what?" Temple said, frowning from across the table as he slouched back in his chair, his iron gray eyes glassy from the cheap but potent hooch. "You don't think the five of us could take him down?"

"Oh, maybe you could," Thornton said, not wanting to seem overconfident. Bounty killers worked best when they had something to prove. "But it ain't really the breed I care about." He turned to Temple, hardening his jaws and gritting his teeth. "What I want is the whore. Alive."

Thornton had considered sending more men after Henry and Faith months ago, but he'd nixed the idea. Doubtless, the half-breed would have beefed the others, too, and left Thornton that much poorer and just as desolate.

But if anyone could kill the breed and bring Faith back to the roadhouse where Thornton could punish the wayward whore in all the ways he'd been dreaming about for the past two years, it was these hard-eyed killers gathered before him now.

"Well, that's just damn insultin'," Manley said, staring hard at Thornton as he leaned forward in his chair and dropped his right hand beneath the table.

Temple, sitting to Manley's right, grabbed the man's arm. "Pull your horns in, Kooch.

He's playin' us, tryin' to keep his price down."

Thornton chuckled and let another brief silence fill the room beneath the warming stove's creaks and sighs.

"A thousand for each of you," he said suddenly. "Half now, half when you've brought the whore back . . . alive."

"Alive?" Benny Freeze said, chuckling drunkenly. "Ain't sure Temple can —"

"Shut up!" the group's ramrod said out the side of his mouth, keeping his gray eyes on Thornton. "Where is she?"

"A drummer I know saw them in Arizona. A place called Saber Creek. They were filling a supply wagon, so my guess is they have a place in the sticks."

"That's a fair lot o' ground to cover." Temple grinned and looked at Thornton from beneath his dark brows, the cross tattoo rising on his forehead. "Fifteen hundred apiece. Half now, half when we've brought the whore back fresh as a spring daisy."

Thornton opened his mouth to respond, but Temple cut him off by holding up his hand. "*And* you forget this hog tripe about Wendell Myers. I'll probably kill the son of a bitch *because* he's a son of a bitch, but I don't see how he's worth a special trip up north in the wintertime."

Thornton kept his face calm as he stared back at the head bounty hunter. But his pulse squawked in his ears. He had a quick, flashing vision of slowly carving Faith up with a dull butcher knife, and he could already feel life, like a healing elixir, trickle back into his fetid, green-rotting soul, killing the razor-toothed rat in his belly.

"Deal."

Before Thornton could drink to it, Kooch Manley leaped to his feet with surprising swiftness for a man of his middling years and size. *"Holy shit!"* In a blur of motion, the man grabbed his revolver from his thigh and leveled it just above Thornton's head.

"What the hell?" Thornton cried, ducking down in his chair and folding his arms over his head.

Manley's Remington roared three times in quick succession, sounding like a cannon echoing off the hall's cold, silent walls.

Thornton lowered an arm to peer at the back of the room. A cat-sized rat lay on its back at the base of the carpeted stairs. The varmint had been blown nearly in two. All four feet jerked as it died.

A hushed silence fell over the room. Behind Thornton, Benny Freeze giggled like a girl.

"I ain't seen a rat that size in years," Manley grumbled, slowly lowering his pistol and sinking back down in his chair.

Thornton shuttled his gaze from the rat to the middle-aged bounty hunter, surprise and appreciation for a well-placed shot mixing with the indignation at having more bullet holes in his roadhouse. Frank Miller began chuckling then, too, and he opened his mouth to speak but stopped suddenly, his eyes rising to the ceiling over the bar.

Upstairs, bedsprings sang as though suddenly released, and the patter of quick footsteps sounded. They grew louder until Ruby ran out onto the balcony, holding a buffalo robe around her shoulders.

"Ruby!" Thornton barked.

The girl stopped abruptly, casting her frightened gaze over the balcony rail and into the saloon hall below. She held the robe closed at her throat with one hand while holding the rail with the other. Her brown breasts poked out of the robe's partially open front — heavy and brown nippled.

"Mr. Bill?" the girl said softly, frowning curiously as she slid her eyes from Thornton to the hard-faced gents sitting around him.

"I told you to stay in your room," Thornton said with a defeated air, aware that all pairs of eyes behind him were directed at the balcony.

He pinched the bridge of his nose between his thumb and index finger as Frank Miller whooped loudly and, pushing his chair back so hard it fell over with a slam, leaped to his feet.

"You done lied, Mr. Bill!" the fiery-eyed blond bellowed as he sprinted toward the stairs. "That there's a doxie if I ever seen one!"

Ruby gave a clipped, horrified scream, eyes popping wide. She wheeled and sprinted back the way she'd come.

Miller took the steps three at a time, laughing, pulling himself up the stairs with one hand on the scarred rail. The girl's running feet drummed in the ceiling above the bar.

Thornton jerked with a start as another gun barked behind him and left. The slugs seared the air in front of his face before plunking, one after another, into the staircase around Miller's boots and into the rail a mere inch behind his hand.

Wood slivers flew as the cutthroat dropped to his knees, his hat tumbling off his shoulder. Cowering against the sudden fusillade, he turned a shocked, indignant look over his shoulder, a lock of blond hair hanging like a bird's wing over a cold blue eye.

"What the — ?"

Behind Thornton, Lowry Temple sat with a long-barreled, silver-plated revolver extended over the table, smoke curling from the barrel. He bunched his lips angrily and canted his head toward Thornton. "Pay the man."

The blond scowled. "Huh?"

"Thornton doesn't give away his girls for free," Temple said reasonably. "And no man in my party takes a woman against her will." He glanced at Thornton, and added, "Or the will of her pimp."

Rage kindling in his crazy eyes, Miller glanced around at the quarter-sized holes in the steps and in the railing around him. "You coulda killed me, ya crazy —"

Temple's revolver barked once more, causing all the men, including Thornton, to nearly jump out of their chairs. The bullet smashed into the step about six inches left of the blond's left knee.

"Pay the man."

"For chrissakes!" Miller shoved a hand into his coat, digging around in the breast pocket of his shirt. "How much?"

Thornton just stared at him until Temple turned to him, both brows arched with incredulity, his voice now pitched with impatience, like a schoolmaster dealing with the antics of idiot children. "How much for the whore?"

Thornton wanted to tell the killer that the girl wasn't for sale, but he no longer felt as passionate about it. His mind was on the prospect of Faith and Yakima Henry being hunted down like mangy coyotes by Lowry Temple.

He hesitated, shrugged. He grabbed a split log from the wood box and leaned forward to toss it into the stove.

"Six bits oughta cover it."

CHAPTER 3

Yakima Henry bolted out of a deep sleep with a startled grunt and grabbed the Winchester Yellowboy repeater that he always kept lying across a chair beside his bed. He rammed a shell into the chamber, the shrill metallic rasp shredding the night's dense silence, and aimed the gun at his bedroom door — a vague rectangular shape in the darkness.

His woman, Faith, gasped as she shot up from her own pillow beside him. "What is it?" Her hushed voice trembled slightly as she whispered, "Apaches?"

Breathing hard but holding the Winchester steady, Yakima stared at the door. He'd fought Apaches enough here at his small horse ranch at the base of Bailey Peak, in Arizona Territory, that he expected the door to burst open and for a screaming, painted brave to bound toward him with a war hatchet raised above his head.

But the door remained a solid black rectangle in the wall before him. He frowned. There was only the sound of his and Faith's breathing, the light scrape of the night breeze brushing a weed against the outside cabin wall.

Yakima wasn't sure what he'd heard, if anything. It could have been a dream. But then a shrill, bugling whinny rose in the distance, starting high and slowly dropping until it faded off to silence. It was answered a moment later by the near clatter of corral rails, the scuffle of prancing hooves, and the sudden, screeching, angry wail of Yakima's own black stallion, Wolf.

Yakima cursed and depressed the rifle's hammer.

"The broom tail?" Faith said darkly.

"Sounds like him, don't it?"

Yakima laid the Yellowboy across the chair, threw the covers back, and dropped his bare feet to the floor with a weary groan. Then he dug his heels into the floor and pushed himself off the bed, stiff and sore right down to his bones. He'd spent all the previous day digging a new well behind the cabin, and he was nowhere near ready to leave the mattress sack. Sweeping his long black, sleep-tussled hair back from his face, he grabbed his balbriggans off a wall hook.

"The son of a bitch is back for the mares."

Faith yawned loudly. "That horny bastard." She scuttled out of bed, making the pine posts and woven leather springs creak, and began stumbling around, gathering her clothes. "Thank God it's not Apaches — I'm not ready to meet them yet. But if that stallion runs off those mares and colts again . . ."

"It'll take us another week to get 'em back." Yakima pulled on his worn blue denims over his balbriggans and, breathing hard, his long hair jostling across his shoulders, sat on the bed to pull on his moccasin boots. "He's bound and determined to lead the whole damn remuda down to Mexico!"

"What is it about you men?" Faith growled, dropping a chemise down over her naked breasts. "How many women do you think you need, anyway?"

Yakima grabbed her, drew her to him quickly, enjoying the feel of her breasts mashing against his chest through the thin chemise. "One's good enough for me."

He kissed her and let her go.

"Yeah?"

Yakima chuckled dryly. "More than enough."

Grabbing her denims off a chair back, Faith punched him with the back of her fist.

"Bastard!"

Yakima grabbed the Yellowboy and a handful of .44 shells and headed out the bedroom door, grumbling as he moved through the dark cabin toward the front. He left his hat and jacket on the kitchen wall hooks, in spite of its being fall, with the mountain nights having turned downright brittle. He flung the door open angrily and stepped out onto the porch.

He'd dropped one foot off the top porch step when the broom-tail bronc loosed his tooth-gnashing whinny once again. It swirled as though from all directions, breaking off at the end in a series of knickers and coughing grunts and the clack of a kicked stone.

"Where are you, you son of a bitch?"

Two peeled log corrals and a low, log-and-stone stable sat kitty-corner from the cabin. Yakima's blaze-faced black stallion, Wolf, was running in circles, bobbing his head wildly, his sleek black mane glistening in the shimmering starlight. The mares and foals were dancing around the adjacent stable, the foals skitter-stepping close to their nickering mothers.

Their hoof thuds rang clear in the cool, dry, silent night.

Around the cabin, the stable, the corrals,

and the windmill that squawked softly above the stone water tank at its base, pine- and fir-stippled hills and low, rocky ridges humped, silhouetted against the starry sky and the black velvet mountain walls rising in all directions beyond the clearing.

The wild bronc bugled his crazed call once more. Yakima turned his gaze to the bluff rising north of the cabin. A silhouette moved at the top of the bluff, amongst the tall firs and pines and cabin-sized boulders.

Boots ground gravel in the yard, and someone said, "The bronc again?"

Yakima glanced to his left. Faith's younger brother, Kelly, was moving out from the stable, tucking his shirt into his pants, holding a rifle under his right arm. The kid still hadn't regained his weight after his six-month stint in a Mexican prison from which Yakima and Faith had sprung him, and his angular shadow slid along the rocky ground beside him. His breath jetted in the air around his head.

"It ain't Santa Claus."

Kelly stopped before the cabin, lifting his chin to listen. He wore an overlarge sheepskin vest on his narrow shoulders. "You see him?"

Yakima stared at the silhouette, which was frozen now. He felt the bronc staring back at him with challenge.

"Think so." Yakima moved off the porch steps and began jogging north. Behind him, boots thumped and there was the rasp of a rifle's cocking lever as Faith ran onto the porch.

Staring straight ahead as he ran, Yakima said, "Faith, you and Kelly stay here in case he circles around on me again."

"You want us to shoot him if we see him?" Faith called, a reluctant note in her voice.

Yakima didn't like shooting horses any more than she did. In fact, he'd always gotten along better with horses than with most people he'd run into. But the broom-tail stud was wreaking havoc with his still-fledgling ranch operation, and if the stallion had his way, Yakima would end up with no ranch at all.

"Kill the bastard!" he called over his shoulder as he ran north through the sage and piñons.

He held the Yellowboy in both hands across his chest. Leaping stones and brush clumps, he bolted up the slope, huffing and puffing against the quickly steepening grade. A hundred yards straight above him, beside a lightning-topped fir at the top of the ridge, the stallion held his ground, breath jetting from his nostrils — a nightmarish silhouette against the glinting, starry sky.

Watching Yakima run toward him, the horse nickered angrily, snorting, bobbing his head, and clawing gravel. His black eyes glistened demonically.

Yakima took his rifle in one hand and grabbed a juniper branch with the other, pulling himself up a steep shelf between the shrub and a fan of slide rock. "I'm comin', you son of a bitch."

Just beyond the talus, he stopped, bending forward to catch his breath. The horse stood frozen again, staring down at him from forty yards away. Yakima grinned. The horse flicked its tail — a fanlike shadow moving behind him.

Yakima was downwind of the bronc, and he could smell the horse's gamey, sagey scent — the wild aromas of Southwestern mesas and canyons and lost, nameless barrancas in which no man save Apaches and maybe a few conquistadores had ever stepped foot.

Slowly, a snarl belying his own reluctance at shooting something so raw and untrammeled, he raised the rifle to his shoulder. He glanced down to be sure of his footing, then dropped to one knee. The movement hadn't taken him much over two seconds, but when he raised his head again to sight down the Yellowboy's barrel, the place beside the lightning-topped fir was filled only with stars sprinkled like sugar on a black table.

The bronc had disappeared as though he'd never been there at all. Hoof thumps rose from the other side of the ridge, quickly fading.

Yakima lowered the Yellowboy and cursed.

Last time the horse had visited the ranch, it had led Yakima away from the yard, then circled around from another direction. That time, the mares had broken out of their corral and trailed the stud into the desert twenty miles south. It had taken Yakima, Kelly, and Faith a good week to retrieve the scattered band, and they'd lost a foal to a mountain lion.

Yakima gained the ridge crest where the bronc had been standing, and cast his gaze down the other side. The wild stallion was a jostling silhouette retreating toward the bottom of the ridge directly below Yakima's position, meandering through the pines with its tail up, its hoof thuds rising dully.

The half-breed, frustration edging aside his reluctance, snapped the rifle to his shoulder. He fired three quick shots, the reports flatting out across the ridges, the slugs plunking into rocks and pine limbs.

The bronc whinnied and faded into the darkness at the bottom of the ridge.

Yakima knew where the horse was heading; he bolted left across the ridge crest to head him off. Down the ridge's south end he plunged, tripping on a root and falling and rolling once before he leaped to his feet once more and continued down the slope. Fleet as an antelope he ran, the moccasins nearly soundless on the gravelly, weed-tufted terrain. Dodging pines and crossing two more hills and another steep ridge, he stood atop a rocky bluff and stared into an ink-black canyon yawning on the other side.

The cold air raked in and out of his lungs, burning.

Holding his rifle across his rising and falling chest, he narrowed an eye, pricking his keen ears, waiting.

Faith's voice rose faintly behind him. "Yakima?"

He continued to stare into the canyon, listening for the horse. But there was only the slight rustle of the breeze against the pine boughs and boulders, the faraway yap of coyotes.

The broad canyon before him yawned blackly. Beyond stood the high, snub-peaked Sunset Ridge mantled in flickering starlight.

The bronc must be circling, intending to head back to the ranch from the base of Bailey Peak. Smart son of a bitch.

Yakima lowered the rifle and loosed a long sigh. He'd just started to turn and head back down the ridge when he smelled the faint but unmistakable musk of horse sweat and sagebrush.

His pulse quickened. He started to raise the rifle once more. Before he could get the barrel leveled, a large black mass bolted out from behind a thumb of rock and shrubs on his left.

Eyes blazing starlight and fury, the sleek coyote dun rose onto its rear hooves with a bugling scream that echoed inside Yakima's skull, blurring his vision and rattling his eardrums. There was no time for a shot.

Yakima dropped the Yellowboy and flung himself toward the canyon. A half second later, the horse's front hooves plunged into the ground where the half-breed had been standing, kicking rocks and gravel.

Propelled by his own momentum, Yakima rolled toward the canyon's vast black mouth. The bronc continued screaming and bucking, flailing its front hooves, intent on grinding Yakima to a fine powder.

One blow glanced off Yakima's right calf

while another grazed his back with an eye-watering slice of stone-sharpened hoof. As the horse rose once more, screaming, its front legs curved like scythes, Yakima rolled farther toward the canyon. His gut fell when his legs slid over the edge.

Desperately, he clawed at the ground with both hands but to no avail. The rest of his body followed his legs, until only his head poked up above the lip of the ridge.

He reached for a rock knob, caught it, began to pull himself up. The knob crumbled.

"Shit!" His stomach surged into his throat as he slid straight down the canyon wall, the rock raking him painfully as he flailed with his moccasin boots and hands for a hold.

A stout root shot up under his arm and he didn't so much grab the root as the root grabbed him — a stop so violent that for a second he thought his arm had been torn from its socket. Beneath the arm, the root squawked like overstrained hemp. Grabbing it with both hands, grunting and sighing, sweat popping from every pore, he dug his fingers into the root while gravity seemed to be pulling him toward the canyon, like a thousand-pound anvil tied to each ankle.

He tried to dig his moccasin toes into the

rocks, but he could find no crack or fissure wide enough. Above his grunts, groans, and pants, he heard the drumming of horse hooves. He figured it was the bronc doing a victory dance atop the ridge.

Then Faith's warmly familiar, reassuring voice yelled, "Yakima?"

"H-here," he grunted, grinding his fingers into the root while feeling as though his swollen knuckles were tearing slowly apart. "Here!"

Hooves clomped atop the ridge. A horse snorted. Faith's voice again: "Where?"

Yakima gritted his teeth as his sweat-slick fingers slipped off the root. Wincing, he renewed his hold, trying to grab the root as close to the canyon wall as possible.

He sucked a breath and used it to call as loud as he could, "Down here!"

It was too dark for her to see him, so she'd have to locate him by his voice.

"Down here!" he yelled, louder. "Throw a ro—"

Without warning, the root snapped with a cracking *pop.* He shot straight down the canyon wall like a stone.

CHAPTER 4

"Christ!" Yakima rasped, gritting his teeth as he raked his hands along the canyon wall rolling up in front of him like a fast-flowing river seen from above — a blur of shadows and starlit rock and small tufts of wiry brown brush.

He kicked at the wall, desperately searching for another hold.

His moccasins nudged something and slipped on past it. His hands grabbed it — a lip of rock two or three inches wide.

Faith called from above, her voice so shrill with terror she sounded angry. *"Yakima?"*

He dug at the rock ledge with his fingers, sweat bathing his face and pasting his underwear top to his chest. He ground his teeth together and managed a wry, taut "Yes, dear?"

"Where *are* you?"

He kicked at the canyon wall, searching for any hold at all. "A few yards farther down from where I was a second ago."

He wasn't sure she'd heard him. He was expending so much energy trying to cling by his fingertips to the narrow rock ledge that he couldn't work up much volume. His stomach sank as his aching fingers began to slip down the curving edge of rock. He continued kicking the wall with his boot toes but found nothing but a sheer rock surface.

"Uhnnnh . . ." He sucked a sharp, shallow breath, his fingers sliding with agonizing certainty down over the dull edge of the rock.

Something slapped his left shoulder and ear with a raking sting.

"Grab the rope!" Faith called.

He glanced to his left. A lariat sloped down the wall above and over his left shoulder. With a curse he channeled his waning strength into his right hand, dug those fingers more firmly into the rock.

He released his left hand from the ledge and grabbed the rope. When he had a hold, he grabbed it with his right hand, too, dropping another foot as his weight ate up the slack.

"Got it?" Faith called.

"Got it!"

Yakima got a good grip on the rope,

clutching it as though to wring water from a towel, and when Faith led the horse forward — she probably had the lariat dallied around the saddle horn — he began to rise, walking slowly up the sheer stone wall.

His hands screeched from grappling with the root and the narrow ledge, and the rope burned into his chafed palms, but he hung on. It was a jerky ride, with the horse pulling, and slowly the ridge came into view above, stars winking beyond the arrow-shaped tops of the pines.

"Yakima?" Faith called again, when he was about ten feet from the ridge crest.

"Keep goin'."

A couple rocks and some gravel broke loose beneath his feet, bouncing and rattling down the wall behind him as he neared the lip, walking up onto the crest as though gaining the top of a staircase.

"Okay." The word rushed out of him on a feeble sigh.

Yakima slumped away from the canyon and dropped to his knees, breathing heavily and massaging his palms. Faith ran up from the far side of the ridge, where she'd stopped her horse in the pines, and dropped down beside him. She threw her arms around his neck and pressed her face to his sweaty cheek.

"Jesus, are you all right?"

Dropping onto his hands and knees, he sucked air as though he'd sprinted a hundred yards. "Little . . . worse . . . for the wear."

Faith had a strong, pretty face with almond-shaped blue eyes framed by thick gold-blond hair. She could give you a look that could make you feel like a copper-riveted fool. "What were you *doing* down there, anyway?"

He chuckled, sat back on his heels, and drew a deep, long breath of cool, high-mountain air. "That damn broom tail's even smarter than I thought he was. Smarter than me, I know that."

"He ran you down there?"

Yakima's face warmed with chagrin, and he shook his head as he glanced at the thumb of rock the bronc had hidden behind. "Bastard drygulched me."

"He is smarter than you."

Faith chuckled dryly, grabbed his hand, and leaned close to inspect his arm. His longhandle top was torn in strips across his chest and shoulders, and bloodied. Through his torn denims, his left knee looked like raw meat.

"We best get you back to the cabin and assess the damage, chump."

"I figured Wolf was the only horse smart enough to pull something like that." Yakima shook his head, still breathing hard and only now beginning to feel the cold sting of his cuts and bruises. "But that little dun could teach Wolf a thing or —"

A rifle shot cut the night. Before its echo had died, two more shots flatted out from the direction of the ranch. Horses whinnied, and there was the distant thunder of stomping hooves.

"That's Kelly!" Faith said.

His heart quickening its pace again, Yakima lurched to his feet and stalked down the grade toward Faith's mare, Crazy Ann, nickering quietly and staring in the direction of the ranch yard. "That damn bronc circled around just like I thought he would!"

"Careful!" Faith rasped, jogging toward him, kicking stones as she descended the ridge.

Yakima jerked the riata free of the apple — he'd retrieve it later — and swung up into the saddle that Faith must have thrown on Crazy Ann in a hurry, using only the rope halter the mare had already been wearing. He held out his left hand. Faith grabbed it, and he swung her easily up behind him and ground his heels against Crazy Ann's ribs.

He put the horse down the slope through the black pine columns. Faith squeezed his arm and said in his ear, "Yakima, don't run her — it's too dark."

Knowing the woman was right, he held the mare back to a jouncing jog until he hit the wagon trail, then swung the horse left and heeled her into a gallop. The trail rose and fell over the fir-studded knobs and Yakima peered ahead, toward the ranch sitting at the base of Bailey Peak, dark and silent beneath the stars.

There was no more gunfire, and he was relieved not to hear the cacophony of rumbling hooves. All he needed was for the mares to break out of the corral and shadow that crazy bronc to hell and back. Wolf would no doubt do the same, as the corral hadn't been built that could hold the stallion when his blood was up — and nothing got his blood up more than competition for his mares.

As Yakima and Faith approached the ranch yard, the half-breed raked his gaze this way and that, glad to find the horses still milling within both corrals. A silhouetted human figure sat atop the mares' corral, near the rails partitioning that corral off from Wolf's. A pinprick of light showed, and then Yakima caught a whiff of tobacco smoke.

"Thank God," Faith said as the half-breed turned the mare toward the corrals. "They're all here."

Yakima drew the mare up to her brother. Kelly was smoking a quirley atop the corral while scratching Wolf's ears as the black stallion held his head near the kid, who, at nineteen years old, was three years younger than his sister and, like his sister, had a natural flare for horses.

Yakima felt lucky to have Kelly kicking around the ranch, helping out until he could decide where he wanted to go and what he wanted to do with his life. The boy's time in the Mexican prison, where he'd been held by a rogue rurale captain on trumped-up charges, had taken a toll on him mentally as well as physically.

"What were you shootin' at?" Yakima asked him.

Kelly hooked a thumb over his shoulder. "Just like you said, he circled around again."

"You put a bullet in him?"

"Nah." Kelly shrugged. "I ain't much of a shot, and he didn't give me much of a target, weaving around them pines. I think I scared him pretty good, though. I've been listening for him, but I haven't heard a thing. Less'n he's just waitin' out there."

The kid, who had longish hair nearly the same color as his sister's, and an angular, handsome face, gestured with his quirley at Yakima's arm. "Looks like you tangled with a bobcat."

"Nope." Faith slid fleetly straight back off the mare's rear. "The bronc pitched him over the ridge."

"Jumpin' Jesus! He's devilish, ain't he?"

"The horses around here are some smarter than I am — I know that. I walked right up to him like a damn rube." Yakima swung down from the saddle, shucked Wolf under the stallion's chin, and began leading the mare around the corral toward the stable. "Let's get some sleep. We'll ride out after that fork-tailed son of a bitch at first light."

Kelly quickly field-stripped his brown paper cigarette and jumped off the corral. "I'll put her away, Yakima. You best get inside and let my sister tend them cuts. She got good at doctoring at the home ranch in Wyoming, all them many years ago."

"All them many years ago," Faith said jeeringly. She wasn't yet twenty-three, but it did feel like a lifetime ago since she and Kelly had grown up in the Chugwater Buttes north of Cheyenne.

"I'm all right," Yakima said. "I'm gonna

check —"

"Get in there, chump," Faith said, striding up behind him and pushing him toward the cabin. "Before you bleed dry."

Yakima gave a wry chuff and, while Faith tugged playfully on his arm, tossed the mare's reins to Kelly. "You know what?"

He wheeled, stooped forward, and pulled Faith over his shoulder, lifting her off her feet.

She gave a startled shriek, laughing. "Yak-i-*ma!*"

"You're bossy!"

"You need a boss. Now, put me down before you kill us both!"

"Hush."

As he carried her toward the cabin, Faith punching him and feebly complaining, she called to Kelly, "Rub down Crazy Ann — will you, little brother? I rode her kind of hard out to rescue this worthless man of mine!"

Yakima laughed both with relief that he still had his horses and at Faith's creative oaths — the girl could curse like a seasoned Irish freighter — as he kicked the cabin door open and hauled the young woman inside and set her brusquely down on the hard-packed earthen floor.

"Idiot!"

Faith swatted his shoulder and grabbed his hand to inspect his arm once more, leaning close to see in the dim light of the lamp she'd lit before leaving the cabin.

Yakima turned toward her, wrapped his good arm around her waist, and crouched to tip her head back and kiss her. She resisted, pushing away from him, but then she relented, opening her mouth for him. She smiled, chuckling, and pushed away abruptly, shaking her hair back from her eyes.

"How many stallions am I going to have to wrestle tonight?" she asked.

"I'll let you know."

"Get in there," Faith ordered, gesturing toward the door leading down a short hall to their bedroom. "I'll bring some water and bandages. Shuck out of those longhandles. I'll darn and patch 'em tomorrow."

"Good woman!" Yakima grabbed a bottle off a kitchen shelf and headed into the dark hall toward the open door of their room.

When Faith and Kelly had come here to live with him, after their Mexican adventure, he'd added two rooms to the back of the cabin — a bedroom for him and Faith and, in the event she might become in the family way, another room for a child. He didn't voice his reason for the second room to

Faith. They'd only been together a few months — too short a time to talk about raising a family — but, just the same, he silently hoped she would stay and that they would raise a family together in the years ahead.

Another reason he didn't mention the reason for the second room was that he didn't want to make her feel boxed in. Faith had been a sporting girl for many years, and in spite of living in relative imprisonment by her last employer, Bill Thornton, she'd been a free, independent spirit all her life, as a hard upbringing either breaks you or sets you free.

Maybe she wasn't ready to settle down for the long haul. Maybe she never would be.

Maybe Yakima himself wasn't ready to settle down yet, either. He'd been alone since his mixed-blood Indian mother had died when he was only twelve; his German gold-hunting father had died several years before that. And while loneliness had haunted him as he'd straddled the netherworld between races, ostracized by both white men and Indians, loneliness and self-reliance had become a way of life.

Until a few months ago, it had been just him and his horses. He hoped he continued to feel the way he did now — ready to settle down and grow old with a good woman. He'd just turned thirty, and he wasn't getting any younger, and the older he'd grown, drifting alone, the lonelier he'd become.

A life should be shared.

Yakima lit a lamp on the dresser — one of the few store-bought pieces of furniture and one he'd hauled by wagon from Saber Creek nearly forty miles away after Faith and Kelly had moved in. He shucked out of his balbriggans and was about to settle into the bed until he looked at his bloody arm and leg, and reconsidered. He sank instead into the hide-bottomed, stag-horn chair beside the bed.

The cool air drifting through the open window dried the sweat on his skin, gave him a slight, refreshing chill and caused the cuts and scrapes to burn slightly. As Faith's boots thumped in the hall and water sang quietly in a tin basin, he uncorked the whiskey bottle, splashed a finger into a tin cup on the dresser beside him, and threw it back.

Faith turned through the door, and, moving with purpose, set the basin atop the dresser and opened the dresser's second drawer. She produced a small purple bottle, uncapped it, and shook a couple of drops into the basin.

58

"What's that?" Yakima asked, his voice raspy from the whiskey he'd bought for fifty cents in Saber Creek.

"Shadbark powder mixed with balsam-root. Old whore's cure. Don't know what it does exactly, but we old whores use it for everything."

She dropped the bottle back into the dresser, then brought the basin over to Yakima's left side. She set it on the floor, knelt beside it, and squeezed the water from the sponge.

As she began dabbing at his arm, he reached over with his right hand and slid a handful of hair back from her forehead, and growled admonishingly, "Don't say that."

She didn't look up but continued cleaning the cut as she said quietly, "My old profession . . . it doesn't bother you?"

After Yakima had helped her escape from Thornton's Roadhouse, she'd run her own pleasure parlor in the mining camp of Gold Cache. That was before she came down here looking for Yakima to help her spring her brother from the Mexican prison, and stayed.

"I never think about it. Any more than I think about what I've done, gettin' by."

She squeezed the bloody water from the sponge and continued dabbing at the congealed blood welling from the cuts. She glanced up at him now, the lamplight flickering in her large blue eyes and casting small shadows across her heart-shaped face and her neck with the small, heart-shaped birthmark. "You ever think about Ace?"

Ace Cavanaugh, the gambler she'd married in Gold Cache and who'd been killed by rurales in Mexico.

Yakima splashed another finger into his cup and shook his head. "Nope."

She studied him as her hand continued to work automatically, her eyes searching his, suspiciously probing all his secrets. Finally, the corners of her full mouth rose, and she took the cup out of his hand, sipped, and handed it back to him.

Her eyes watered slightly from the whiskey rolling down her throat, and her voice was husky as she said, "We're doing pretty well, aren't we, Yakima? Considering where we both came from. . . ."

Staring down at her, caressing her smooth cheek with the backs of his brown fingers, Yakima nodded. "Fine as frog hair."

She smiled brightly then, her eyes flashing. She lowered her head and continued to work in silence, moving from his arm to his leg as he sat there naked in the chair, sipping the whiskey to ease the stinging pain and feeling himself grow aroused by his woman's touch.

When she'd finished wrapping the wounds with strips of torn sheets, she glanced at his belly, and smiled once more through the strands of hair in her eyes.

She wrapped her hand around him, squeezed.

"Sometimes," she whispered, "it's an advantage . . . keepin' house with an experienced woman."

She caressed him gently, then slowly lowered her head, her blond hair spilling across his groin.

Yakima squeezed the chair arms and groaned.

CHAPTER 5

In spite of the whiskey and his woman's soothing ministrations, Yakima didn't sleep well the rest of the night. He'd endured plenty worse scrapes and bruises than those he'd acquired in his tumble down the canyon wall. But his mind turned every coyote yap and owl hoot into the stallion's challenging bugle.

He, Faith, and Kelly were up before dawn, as the others hadn't slept any better than he had. Faith whipped up a quick breakfast of side pork, fried potatoes, and strong black coffee, and they ate by the light of a hurricane lamp, the crackling cookstove pushing the night's cold out of the kitchen.

After breakfast, Yakima and Kelly saddled up and slid rifles into their saddle scabbards.

It was time to take care of the broom-tail bronc once and for all, before the hot-blooded stallion wreaked any more havoc on the ranch, or the Bailey Peak Outfit, which was the name the half-breed had burned into the wooden portal at the edge of the yard. He thought the handle gave the place, so recently carved from the rocks, sage, and pines, some authenticity and respectability. Since Faith and Kelly had come, it had become more than just a bunkhouse; it was now a real home.

It deserved a name.

As Yakima finished double-checking his saddle cinch, Faith stepped out of the cabin swinging a burlap sack. "Here's your grub, in case you're not back by noon."

"Obliged." Yakima took the sack, glanced over his shoulder at Kelly, who was still fiddling with his rifle scabbard, then wrapped a muscular arm around Faith's waist, bent her slightly back, and gave her a quick but passionate kiss on the mouth. She returned the kiss, laughing and tugging on his long hair falling around his shoulders.

Pulling away from her, Yakima swung up onto the black's hurricane deck. "I hope to be back by noon. Something tells me that bronc's stayin' close. He's got a good whiff of those mares, and he likes what he smells."

Shivering, Faith hunched her shoulders inside the buckskin coat she'd donned against the morning's sharp chill. The cabin's chimney lifted gray smoke behind and above her. "You two be careful."

She'd wanted to ride along, but Yakima had convinced her to remain at the ranch in case the bronc returned.

The boy and Yakima put their horses into jogs across the yard and out through the wooden ranch portal. In the sage- and pine-studded buttes beyond, they heeled the mounts into lopes, hooves thudding, dust rising in the wan dawn light behind them.

Faith remained on the porch, watching their jostling figures disappear in the purple shadows. When they were gone, she turned toward the corral.

The mares were milling about with their foals, a couple of which were milking, and staring at Faith expectantly. It was still a half hour early for the morning feeding, but Faith said, "All right, ladies. Since we've eaten, I guess it's only fair you and the children eat. . . ."

She let her sentence trail off, frowning at her claybank mare, Crazy Ann, who stood pricking her ears southward, as though she heard something in the far distance.

Faith turned to peer across the broad, hilly meadow in which the ranch sat, and along the faint horse trail stretching south toward a stand of dark pines and blue mountains beyond. It was the trail that angled down the foothills and across the desert to the town of Saber Creek, thirty miles away.

"What is it, Ann?"

Faith stared in the direction the mare was gazing for a time, wondering if the broomtail stallion was out there somewhere, stalking just beyond the limits of her own vision and hearing, waiting for another chance to strike.

But, as far as she could tell, there was nothing but a slight breeze ruffling the sage and broom grass. Crazy Ann, whom Faith had named after seeing the mare's crazy stare and quirky, fidgety corral dance, as though she were imagining unseen predators, was probably only hearing her own wild conjurings.

Faith went inside for her work gloves and her man's felt Stetson, which she thonged beneath her chin, then headed back outside. Drawing her hair into a loose ponytail, she crossed the yard to the corral. A couple of the mares, realizing it was time for breakfast, whinnied happily, and the foals nickered like lambs, bolting into playful runs, nipping at the other foals' ears and backsides. Even Crazy Ann came to the fence, and Faith was relieved.

She knew the broom tail needed to be

taken down, but she didn't want to have to do it herself.

Faith fed a coffee tin of oats to each mare and foal, and tried to keep the more aggressive mares out of the others' feed, then pitched fresh bluestem hay from the cribful that Kelly had cut down by the stream while Yakima had dug the new well. She enjoyed being in the corral with the horses, checking the foals for ear mites and tics and doctoring with turpentine and mud the nips the contrary mares sometimes inflicted on one another.

She'd enjoyed ranch work when she'd been growing up in the Chugwater Buttes, though her and Kelly's father had been a brooding, arbitrary man, given to the whip and the bottle. It felt good to return to such work in the open air again after the half dozen years she'd spent working in saloons and brothels.

She didn't feel guilty about those years. For girls who'd found themselves alone on the frontier, as she had when her father had turned her out after her mother had died, there were few other alternatives save starving to death. But she knew it had condemned her to a certain cynicism and darkness, a certain callousness. And she sometimes wondered, even when she was making love with Yakima, enjoying working in the cabin or out here in the stable and corral, if her past would leave her in peace.

She hoped with all her soul that her luck would hold, that her happiness would endure — that the Fates would continue to allow her to enjoy her life out here with a good man whom she loved with all her heart.

When she'd filled all the stock tanks with water from the windmill, hauling the buckets on an oak pole draped across her shoulders, she gathered tack in need of mending from the stable. It was now nine o'clock, judging by the sun kiting high and lens-clear above Bailey Peak. She'd spend the rest of the morning mending and oiling tack, but first she'd put on a fresh pot of coffee to help leach the autumn chill from her bones.

She wished Yakima were here. She and the half-breed and Kelly had formed the stockman's custom of midmorning and midafternoon coffee, kicked back in chairs on the cabin's front porch. It helped break up the often grueling albeit satisfying ranch work that left them all exhausted by sundown.

A slight breeze picked up, shepherding a tumbleweed into her path as she crossed from the stable to the cabin. She kicked the weed away, squinting against the dust, then turned suddenly toward the south, peering beyond the meadow toward the far line of trees showing spruce green now in the cool, crystal mountain sunlight.

She'd heard something. A clipped voice on the breeze and possibly the rattle of a bit chain.

Crazy Ann nickered behind Faith. Feeling a cricket of apprehension skitter up her spine, she stood staring for a minute, shading her eyes with her free hand. She half expected the wild stallion to come barreling over those knobs, stepping high and buck-kicking, head down, his dun mane blowing.

After last night, she wouldn't put it past the horse to lead Yakima and Kelly a half day's hard ride from the ranch, then circle back for the mares he'd set his hat for.

But there was nothing out there but the sunlight and rolling, sage-covered knobs and the line of thick pine forest beyond. Beyond them, mere shadows this time of the day, distant ranges rolled up like fog between here and Mexico.

She continued striding to the cabin but stopped again suddenly when Crazy Ann and another mare whinnied almost in unison. Now there was something moving amidst the pines and firs, bobbing slightly above the sage. Her heart quickening, Faith lifted a shading hand once more.

Not something.

Someone.

Riders galloped toward her, rising and falling with the swell of the land, moving out of the pines at the edge of her vision and out of sight behind a high, thimble-shaped butte. She'd only caught a momentary look, but there appeared to be five or six riders — white men, not Apaches. Sunlight flashed off steel.

Faith felt a tightness in her shoulders. She turned with forced calm toward the cabin, stepped up onto the porch, and strode inside, where she dropped the tack on the kitchen table and grabbed her Winchester rifle off the deer antler rack on the living room wall.

As she turned toward the door, which she'd left standing ajar behind her, she racked a fresh shell into the Winchester's breech and stepped back outside, turning on the porch to face south.

Hoof thuds rose clearly now as five riders loped toward her along the trail, a hundred yards away and closing. Watching them come, Faith cocked a hip and held the Winchester low across her thighs. Not a very friendly way of greeting newcomers, maybe, but since she was alone here, she wasn't taking any chances.

She studied the men warily — five rough-looking hombres in fur coats, riding good horses bathed in silvery sweat. The lead rider had long black hair like Yakima's, and a black stovepipe hat with a snakeskin band. As he and the others rode even with the stable and continued into the yard, she saw they were well and prominently armed with pistols, knives, and rifles.

Faith had encountered enough such men to know that they were hunters of some sort — market hunters, scalp hunters, or bounty hunters.

She gave a slight, involuntary shiver as the memory of Wit Bardoul swept through her mind — the tracker who'd ghosted her and Yakima into the Rocky Mountains west of Thornton's Roadhouse in Colorado, and whose intention was to kill them and bring their heads back to Thornton for the bounty.

Faith drew a deep breath as she watched the riders approach the cabin, fanning out in a semicircle as they closed on the porch, the mares nickering in the corral behind them, and the colts running in circles, kicking.

The strangers reined their mounts to a stop about thirty yards from the front porch and sat their tired mounts round shouldered and staring at Faith. She stared back at them, frowning, that cricket of apprehension now fluttering up and down her spine in earnest.

The lead rider, who wore a cross tattoo in the middle of his forehead, suddenly doffed his stovepipe hat with a flourish and held it over his heart.

"Well, hello there, little lady," he said, grinning. "How are you this fine mountain mornin'?"

CHAPTER 6

"Mornin'."

Faith raked her wary gaze across the five riders sitting their sweaty mounts in front of the porch. They were four white men and a Mexican. All five pairs of eyes stared back at her, faint lascivious sneers stretching chapped, windburned lips.

"Dusty ride," said the leader, swiping his hat across his jeans. "Sure could use a drink of water and a cup of coffee, if you'd see fit to accommodate, ma'am."

Faith sized them up once more, quickly darting her eyes across their guns. "Where you from?"

"Saber Creek." The tattooed leader scrubbed his arm across his forehead, then set the stovepipe hat back down on his head. "Chasin' bank robbers." He hipped around in his saddle to scrutinize the yard. One of the others, a beefy, middle-aged gent, had been looking around the yard as well, as though looking for someone. "Sure could use some belly wash before we head back after 'em. And our horses could use a blow. Wouldn't mind if we tied up here at your hitch rail, would you?"

"Posse from Saber Creek, huh?" Faith said. "Where's Sheriff Speares? He usually leads posses out of Saber Creek himself."

"Broke off north," said a fair-skinned man — short and muscular, with a bull neck and cobalt blue eyes dancing around beneath his tan hat brim. His heated gaze flickered across Faith's body quickly before he turned his head to one side to dribble chaw into the dust beneath his horse.

"Bank robbers, huh?" Faith said, not believing a word of it. "They usually head south toward Mexico."

"Well, maybe these were Canadian bank robbers," chuckled the youngest member of the group, a bucktoothed kid with a sparse goat beard the color of corn silk.

The lead rider leaned forward on his saddle horn, smiling affably, though on such a steely-eyed, weirdly tattooed face, it came off like a sneer. "Invite us in? We'll mind our manners."

Faith didn't know what they wanted. Maybe the horses. Maybe her. But she wasn't letting them into the cabin.

"I can't ask you in," she said, shifting the rifle in her sweat-moist hands but keeping it low against her thighs. "My man's taken ill. Has a fever. Might be catching. You can water your horses and rest right here on the porch. I'll bring you out some coffee."

"What?" the tall Mexican said, scowling beneath the brim of his worn leather slouch hat. "You gonna make us lap it up like stray dogs on the porch?"

Faith held the man's indignant gaze. Squeezing the rifle in both hands, she turned and began slowly moving toward the half-open door behind her. As she glanced back at the strangers, the leader swung deliberately down from his saddle. The others leaped down from their own mounts then, too, the Mexican setting his jaws and snarling.

Heart hammering, Faith bolted over the cabin's threshold, glancing back again as the group's leader ducked under a hitch rail and strode quickly onto the porch, his cold steel eyes riveted on Faith. She grabbed the door handle, swung it closed, and, as the lead rider slammed himself against the other side with a loud, wooden thump, she slammed the locking bolt home.

"Goddamnit!" The man threw his body against the timbered door again, and the stout door shuddered in its frame, making cracking sounds. "Frank, run around back!"

Faith wheeled and, holding the rifle in one hand, ran between the kitchen and living room and into the back add-on. She rushed past her and Yakima's bedroom just as, in the sashed window right off the back door, the bull-necked blond appeared sprinting around the cabin's right rear corner. He'd lost his hat, and his broad, clean-shaven face was flushed, his lips bunched.

Faith screamed as she threw her shoulder up against the door just as the blond tripped the latch with a metallic rattle. Frank pushed the door open, laughing. Faith dropped the rifle, set her boots into the puncheons, and heaved the door back against its frame, then rammed the locking bolt home.

Frank punched the door and cursed. "Open the door, you bitch!"

A whomping thud sounded at the other end of the cabin. Faith wheeled, started back toward the front, stopped, scooped up her Winchester, and continued running. The front door shuddered in its frame as something large and heavy was thrown up against it. A shadow caught her right eye, and she turned to see the fleshy, small-eyed face of the older gent grinning through the kitchen window at her.

As the front door thundered in its frame once more, she held her rifle high in her shaking hands and screamed, *"What do you want?"*

"You, Faith," the leader said tightly, just loudly enough to be heard through the door and above the boot thuds and scrapes on the porch.

As another loud thud sounded against the front door, Faith gritted her teeth and pressed the Winchester's butt to her shoulder. Another thundering *whomp,* and the door flew wide, splinters spraying out from the frame. The long-haired lead rider in the stovepipe hat flung a wood splinter aside and ducked through the door, striding to Faith quickly, his bristly cheeks flushed, his iron gray eyes grim and hard.

"Get out of my house!" she shouted.

She triggered the rifle, and the lead rider's head jerked back and sideways as the bullet drew a red line across his cheek.

The slug tore into the door frame to the right of the tall, hollow-cheeked Mexican entering behind him. The man flinched, grabbing his leather hat and jerking a quick look at the smoking bullet hole in the door.

"Mierda! Puta bitch!"

Behind him, the goat-bearded kid laughed.

76

Faith lowered the rifle to rack a fresh shell, but she'd only ejected the spent one, which clattered to the floor around her boots, before the lead rider was on her. He jerked the rifle out of her hands and tossed it into the kitchen, where it barked off the food preparation counter and clattered onto the floor.

Faith flung a fist toward the lead rider's cut cheek. The man grabbed it, jerked it down, and slammed the back of his other hand against Faith's right cheekbone — a hard, eye-watering slap that threw her straight back and sprawling onto the floor in front of the door to the hall.

He stepped to one side and, scowling down at her, eyes spitting flames of barely restrained fury, jerked off his neckerchief and dabbed at his cheek. He pulled the cloth away to inspect the blood.

"That's no way to treat guests, Miss Faith."

The Mexican brushed past him toward Faith and reached for her arm. She jerked the arm away, scrambled to her feet, and ran stumbling down the hall. She could hear foot thuds and spur chinks behind her, the jeering laughter of the goat-bearded kid.

Faith turned into the bedroom and swung the door toward the frame. She got it only half closed before the Mexican stopped it with his boot, eyeing her darkly through the crack.

"Goddamnit!" Faith screamed, ramming the door once more against the man's boot. "Get out of my house, you sons o' bitches!"

The Mexican threw his shoulder against the door. Faith groaned and fell as the door flew wide, ricocheting off the wall behind it.

The half-breed closed on her, lips stretched back from his teeth, his black eyes roaming up and down her body with goatish lust.

Behind him, the older gent and the kid watched from the open doorway. The stocky blond moved up behind and between them, placing a hand on a shoulder of each, grinning.

"Hey, you better flip her a coin first, Chulo. Don't wanna rile Temple."

A foot in front of Faith — so close she could smell the rancid sweetness of his breath and the leather of the thick vest beneath his deer-hide coat — the half-breed closed his lips, his eyes burrowing into hers. He leaned forward suddenly. Faith shrieked as his big, black-gloved hands closed on her buckskin mackinaw, and then he was jerking the coat up over her head.

Faith struggled against him to no avail —

in a second he flung the coat across the room, set his gloved hands on her shirt, and tore her man's gray shirt and undershirt down the middle, exposing her breasts.

"No!"

"Holy moly!" the kid howled from the doorway. "Look at those!"

"Jesus Christ," growled the older gent, swaggering into the room like a bull into a pen full of heifers. "That's too much woman for you, Chulo. You'd better let me take the green out of her first."

"Yeah, you better whup the green out of her, Kooch!" the kid yelled.

Ignoring the men behind him, the Mexican reached down, grabbed Faith's left arm painfully, and tossed her up onto the bed as though she weighed no more than a doll. She bounced off her back, her hair tearing loose from the ponytail and splaying across her face. The Mex ripped his grubby hat off his head, flung it across the room, and threw himself on top of her.

He pawed her breasts roughly and rammed his fetid mouth down on hers, using his full weight to press her into the corn shuck mattress.

Faith struggled, turning her head away from him, but the man overpowered her. Pawing her breasts with one hand, he held her head by her hair and kissed her harshly, shoving his tongue into her mouth and grinding his groin against hers.

The others whooped and yelled behind him, the kid dancing a jig and raking his spurs across the hard-packed floor.

When the Mexican finally removed his mouth from Faith's, she sucked a deep breath, then spat his tobacco-sweet spit from her lips. He lowered his head to nuzzle and nibble her breasts. Weakly, angrily sobbing, she rammed her fists across his head and shoulders.

Suddenly, the others fell silent. A gun hammer clicked loudly.

Faith looked up. The Mexican froze with his rough cheek against her breast. A long pistol barrel was snugged against the Mexican's ear. Faith followed the arm extending the gun up to the tattooed face of the long-haired leader hovering over the bed.

The leader gritted his teeth as he said tightly, "Chulo, what have I told you about the evils of unwed fornication?"

Chulo turned toward the man angrily. "Back off, Temple. The girl's mine!"

The leader looked at Faith, blood beading along the bullet burn on his cheek. "Miss, do you want to lie with this man?"

Faith sucked a breath and lifted her

head. *"No!"*

The man called Temple grinned and said wryly, " 'Flee also youthful lusts: but follow righteousness, faith, charity, peace, with them that call on the Lord with a pure heart.' Second Timothy, Chapter Two, Verse Twenty-two."

"She's a whore!" Chulo cried.

"Thornton don't want her soiled. And I would say that lyin' with the likes of your mangy Mexican ass would qualify as soilin'."

"What about me?" the older gent said with an indignant air.

Still staring down his gun barrel at Chulo, Temple said, "Doubly so for you, Kooch."

"Ah, shit, Temple — you ruin everything, you know that?"

Breathing hard, Faith stared up at the Mexican sprawled on top of her. Chulo's eyes flicked to the gun aimed at his eye, then to the steel gray eyes of the man aiming it.

"Pull your horns in, Temple," he growled. "I'm getting off your precious whore though I do not understand what good is a whore if we cannot have her."

"Same here," said the thick-necked, wild-eyed blond, staring down at Faith with crossed arms. He shook his head in amazement and chuckled without mirth.

"Temple'd rather *kill* her than *have* her!"

Temple depressed his pistol's hammer and straightened. Chulo glowered at Faith, cursing, as he climbed off her and stood beside the bed, straightening his shirt and adjusting his crotch with a dip of his knees. He cursed once more loudly, regarded Temple with exasperation, then turned on his heel. He pushed past the other men and stomped on out the door.

Temple stared down at Faith, a bizarre half smile on his thin lips and cold gray eyes. " 'Knowing this first, that there shall come in the last days scoffers, walking after their own lusts.' Second Peter, Chapter Three, Verse Three." His lips stretched, widening his grin as he turned to the other three men standing near the door and staring down at Faith hungrily. "Got that from my ma. There never was a more pious whore than Ma. No, sir."

"Go to hell, Temple," the older gent grumbled, dismissing the group's God-fearing leader with an angry toss of his arm. He turned and stomped through the door, and the other two were close on his heels, tossing incredulous glances behind them.

Holding the flaps of her torn shirts over her breasts, blood glistening on the small cut on her right cheek, Faith sat up on the bed and regarded Temple angrily. "Thornton sent you?"

Temple glanced at her breasts, a faint flush rising in his ruddy, dusty cheeks behind the two- or three-day growth of wiry beard stubble. He flicked his inscrutable gray eyes back to her face, smiling that steely smile.

"Where's the breed?"

"None of your business."

His smile in place, Temple nodded.

"Pack a bag," he ordered, giving his pistol an ostentatious twirl before dropping it into its sheath. "We got a long pull ahead."

CHAPTER 7

A little earlier in the morning and about three miles from the ranch yard, Yakima Henry jerked Wolf's reins back suddenly and threw up a hand for Kelly to stop his own horse behind him.

Yakima had heard the dull thud of an unshod hoof on the still morning air, and now he stared straight ahead. Narrowing his eyes, he picked the wild stud out of the rocks and brush clumps of a rise about a hundred yards away. The bronc held its head low, and it moved down the rise through scattered mesquites and pin oaks with that loose-legged, slightly knock-kneed gait of a tired horse.

Yakima didn't take the time to point out the bronc to Kelly. Knowing the horse's senses were keen, he quickly reached forward to grab Wolf's nose and backed him behind some boulders littering the bottom of the narrow canyon that he and Kelly had been following for the past half hour. It was warmer now, and they'd tied their coats behind their saddles and rolled their shirtsleeves up their arms.

Quietly, Kelly backed his own horse with gentle urgings.

Yakima had known the arroyo led to a *tinaja,* a rock pool that collects rainwater. He'd long ago figured the wild stallion was frequenting the pool, as it was the only good water within several square miles.

Dismounting, he dropped Wolf's reins near some buck brush spiking up around the shaded boulders, and quickly shucked his Winchester from its scabbard. He gently racked a shell, off-cocked the hammer, and moved around behind the horses and down the arroyo. Kelly strode along behind him, his own Spencer in his hands, mimicking Yakima's Apache-like stealth, stepping lightly, breathing through his nose, and holding his arms slightly forward from his body, and still.

Both men meandered around rocks until they were twenty feet from where their canyon opened into another, broader one. The stallion had dropped down from the canyon's far ridge and was somewhere out of sight behind the eroded wall to Yakima's and Kelly's right.

Yakima climbed a few feet up the sloping right bank, keeping his head well below the top and angling forward toward the broader intersecting canyon. He dropped down between a boulder with a V-like crack down its middle. Removing his funnel-brimmed cream hat, Kelly hunkered beside him, not saying anything and breathing quietly through his open mouth.

Yakima stared through the boulder's notch, raking his gaze across the sun-flooded canyon ahead. His blood raced when he spied the little broom-tail bronc dropping its head to drink from the *tinaja* nestled in black volcanic rock and junipers about thirty yards to the right of the conflu-ence of the two canyons.

From this angle, Yakima could see nearly all the bronc's lean, muscular body, which was scarred here and there from brush and, likely, territorial battles with other stallions. The coyote dun had a white spot on his left shoulder and one white rear sock. Another small patch of white shone up high on its forehead, close to its ears.

Yakima didn't have much time. While he was up-breeze of the wild stallion, it was only a matter of minutes, maybe seconds, before the wily beast's senses would detect its stalkers.

The half-breed brought the rifle to his shoulder, slowly thumbing the hammer back. He drew a bead on the stallion's shoulder, slid it slightly up and forward to ensure a heart shot.

He squinted down the Yellowboy's brass receiver and oiled barrel, fixing the bead on a small, pale scar in the dusty, sweaty hide about where the horse's heart would be. Drawing a breath in and holding it, he took up the slack in his trigger finger, feeling the curved trigger press into his deerskin glove.

A second passed. Then two . . . three . . . four . . .

In the corner of his left eye, he saw Kelly turn toward him.

Yakima released the breath he'd drawn, drew another, and snugged his cheek against the rifle's walnut stock.

The coyote dun lifted its head suddenly, turned toward Yakima. Yakima's heartbeat quickened. The horse stood frozen, water dribbling down its bristled muzzle to splatter about the rocks. Its ears twitched and its nostrils worked, testing the air. Its brushy, burr-infested tail arced slightly out from its hindquarters to fall straight down toward the black slab of pitted rock it was standing on.

The horse was alone. No others were near.

No mares, no foals, not even another stallion to fight with. Only a few flies weaved the air about its perfect, regal head.

Yakima tried to pull his index finger back against the Winchester's trigger, but the finger wouldn't move.

The horse jerked back suddenly, dark eyes widening, and then it raised its tail and turned away and trotted up a low rise beyond the tank. It turned around a thumb of rock and stunted piñons, and disappeared into another intersecting canyon, the clomp of its unshod hooves echoing softly behind.

Yakima glanced at Kelly, who was scowling at him. Scowling as well, Yakima turned back to the *tinaja,* lying dark and vacant amidst the rocks.

Any rancher in his right mind would have shot that stud bronc when he'd had him in his sights. Such a horse would wreak costly havoc on any ranch operation, especially one as fledgling as Yakima's. Yakima could have tried to catch him, gentle him as Wolf had been gentled, but having two stallions in his cavvy would lead to a different kind of trouble.

Besides, he had nowhere to house the savage beast. Obviously, the stallion couldn't be corralled with Wolf or the mares and foals. Until he could be gentled — *if* he could be gentled — there was the prospect he'd turn Yakima's log, brush-roofed stable into toothpicks and dust in minutes.

Yakima should have shot him. But he hadn't been able to do it. The stallion's only sin was wanting companionship, after all. To live a good life amongst his own.

As he pushed off his knees, Yakima glanced at Kelly and growled, "Just gonna have to figure something else out, I reckon."

Still regarding Yakima skeptically, Kelly gained his feet and followed him back down to the horses. "But what about . . . ?"

Kelly let his voice trail off as a soft crack resounded in the far distance. Yakima stopped at the bottom of the canyon and turned northwest, the direction from which the shot had come. The report echoed flatly in the high, dry air, bouncing around the canyons.

Kelly looked at Yakima. "Hunter?"

Yakima ran his tongue across his lower lip. "Maybe. Brody Harms lives over on Buzzard Butte, and he hunts these ridges."

Harms was an educated loner from Pennsylvania who, stricken with gold fever, had filed a claim a couple of miles from Yakima's ranch. Every once in a while, when the walls of his diggings shack closed in on him too tightly, Harms would appear on the half-

89

breed's doorstep with a venison haunch wrapped in burlap for supper, and a bottle of cactus wine.

Yakima didn't think Harms had fired the shot, however. He'd be breaking rock in the middle of the day, doing his hunting in the early morning or evening.

Apprehension nibbled at the half-breed's gut.

He slipped the Yellowboy into his saddle boot and grabbed Wolf's reins. "Best head home."

Kelly quickly sheathed his own rifle, worry in the young man's eyes, which were the same lilac blue as his sister's. "Faith?"

Yakima swung up onto Wolf's back. "Let's find out."

He turned the horse in the direction from which they'd come, nudging his heels against the stallion's ribs. Kelly followed suit, and they jogged up out of the arroyo and began following an old horse trail over the rolling, chaparral-covered hills.

Nearly an hour after leaving the *tinaja*, both riders rode up and over the last, high ridge. Halfway down the other side, they halted their mounts amidst tall firs in which mountain chickadees peeped.

Yakima stretched his gaze across the large, wind-brushed, sun-splashed hollow below, where his ranch nestled at the foot of Bailey Peak. Smoke rose from the stone chimney on the cabin's right side. Men and horses were milling in front of the porch, two men mounted, two walking toward the corral. Two more walked out the cabin door, one behind the other.

No. Not two men. A man and Faith. She wore her man's Stetson and her buckskin mackinaw, as though she was heading somewhere. The man behind her held his hand out in front of his waist, as though he was holding a gun on her.

Kelly said, "You recognize 'em?"

Yakima's voice was hard. "Nope." He slipped his Winchester from its saddle boot. One-handed, he racked a shell and laid the rifle across his saddle bows.

Yakima froze as he watched two of the strangers enter the corral housing the prancing mares and foals and, holding their rifles in one hand, move around behind the milling horses, working their way toward the stable on the corral's south side.

Near the cabin, Faith shouted something. She took off running toward the corral. The man behind her stuck his foot out, tripping her and sending her sprawling. The two men in the corral opened up with their rifles, shooting into the air over the heads of the mares and the colts.

Yakima bunched his lips and glanced at Kelly. "Let's go!"

He rammed his heels against Wolf's ribs, and the horse lunged into a wind-splitting gallop down the slope, weaving amongst the pines.

In the ranch yard, Faith screamed again. The mares whinnied and the foals nickered and bolted through the open corral gate, their hooves lifting thunder and dust. As the men in the corral continued shooting and shouting, the long-haired man in the stovepipe hat holstered his pistol under his buffalo coat, picked Faith up like a sack of cracked corn, and threw her belly-down over one of the saddled horses tied at the hitch rail.

Yakima's vision swam with fury.

Curling his index finger through the Yellowboy's trigger guard, Yakima bottomed out in the hollow and raced through the last of the pines. Staring toward the yard, he saw that smoke issued not only from the cabin's chimney but from the doors and windows, as well.

Through the smoke he glimpsed orange flames leaping and dancing around inside the cabin. He hunkered low in the saddle as Wolf raced across the clearing, rising and falling over the sage- and cedar-tufted knobs.

He galloped under the ranch portal. The mares and foals raced off to his left in a sifting cloud of adobe-colored dust, pitching and buck-kicking. The two men leaving the corral with their rifles resting on their shoulders turned as one toward Yakima and Kelly.

The burlier of the two glanced toward the cabin. "Company, Temple!"

The man in the stovepipe hat turned from the hitch rail, then shouted something Yakima couldn't hear. He stepped between the horses and shucked a rifle from a saddle boot.

The two men who'd just left the corral dropped to their knees and raised their rifles toward Yakima and Kelly, who flanked him. The other two men near the cabin grabbed rifles of their own, levered shells, and ran away from the horses to get a clear shot.

Yakima extended his Winchester one handed and, hesitating, not wanting to risk hitting Faith, triggered a shot at the two men bearing down at him from in front of the corral.

His slug plunked into the ground before the older, bulkier gent, making him lurch back on his heels. Kelly fired his Spencer, then tossed the rifle down and took his revolver in his right hand.

Smoke and flames began stabbing from the interlopers' rifles, the *pops* and *crack*s echoing around the yard, slugs plunking into the ground around the horses' pounding hooves and sizzling through the air around Yakima's head.

Kelly fired and yelled angrily, angling away from Yakima to head for the cabin. The half-breed triggered his Winchester twice quickly, cocking one handed and heading Wolf toward the two men near the open corral gate.

The burly gent recocked his own Winchester and snarled savagely as he fired.

The slug sliced past Wolf's right ear and clipped the slack of Yakima's buckskin shirt. The other man near the corral — a tall, gaunt Mexican — triggered his own carbine, howling, as though he was having the time of his life.

Yakima squeezed off a wild shot at the man. Hearing Kelly and Faith scream, he whipped his head left to see the young man sag straight back in his saddle. As his roan continued racing toward the cabin, Kelly did a double somersault off the mount's rump, hitting the ground in a broiling cloud of dust.

Yakima had just whipped his head back toward the corral when a slug fired from the direction of the cabin sizzled across his left temple with a grinding burn. He felt his rifle leave his hand, heard it hit the ground beneath Wolf's thumping hooves.

As more bullets sliced the air and drilled the ground around him, Wolf screamed and lurched left, and, his vision dimming, blood dribbling down from his torn temple, Yakima lost his reins and flew back and sideways down the horse's right hip.

His shoulder hit the ground. His ankle barked in misery as his boot toe hung up in the stirrup and the horse whipped him around in a gut-wrenching half circle, plowing dirt and gravel.

Tooth-splintering pain shot up and down Yakima's twisted ankle and leg.

And then, as his vision continued to dim as though clouds were quickly filling the sky, he was vaguely aware of being dragged at a furious clip, and of men shouting, guns barking, bullets pounding the ground around him, and of Faith screaming so shrilly that her voice cracked, *"YAK-I-MAAAAA!"*

CHAPTER 8

Yakima swam up out of a deep sleep to a sharp pain behind his eyes and a coiled rattler flicking its forked tongue at him and rattling.

The rattler was about six feet away from where Yakima lay at the base of a gully's southern ridge. Yakima recognized the gully. He figured it had once served as a springhouse for some long-dead ancient settler; cool, sweet water intermittently filled the cut. When it was not inhabited by water, however, the gully was a haven for snakes — diamondbacks and Mojave greens.

That's where Wolf must have deposited him, although, having passed out while he'd been dragged out of the yard, Yakima remembered little but a vague sensation of falling and landing hard.

The snake bearing down on him now, eyes like flat shotgun pellets, was a Mojave green, the deadliest of desert vipers.

Instinctively, Yakima began reaching toward his hip, and stopped. The snake ratcheted up its rattle and drew taut as a clock spring, lifting its head to strike. From that angle, it would likely sink its fangs into Yakima's cheek.

He breathed a curse and steeled himself for the inevitable bite.

A gun barked — a hollow *pop* that filled the ravine like a shotgun blast, and died suddenly, reverberating in Yakima's eardrums. Yakima jerked with a start, eyes squeezed shut, for an instant believing, nonsensically, that the roar had somehow been the report the snake had made when it had chomped into his cheek and filled his head with poison.

He opened his eyes.

The snake lay stretched partly out before him, coiling and uncoiling madly, its head and six inches of neck lying separate from its body, the head furiously digging its teeth into a pencil-thin mesquite branch.

"Well, what have we here?" a man's voice said.

Yakima lifted his gaze to the lip of the opposite ridge. A stocky, brown-haired, mustached gent in a shabby fawn vest, bowler hat, and checked trousers stood scowling down at him, the old Remington revolver in his hand still smoking. His round, dusty spectacles winked in the waning sunlight.

"Hold on," said his neighbor, the Easterner, Brody Harms.

Holstering the revolver, Harms turned and disappeared from the ravine's lip. He returned a few seconds later leading a mule by its bridle and glancing down at Yakima again, as though making sure that Yakima was still there or hadn't died, then grabbed his lariat from his saddle.

Quickly, Harms dallied the end of the lariat around the horn, then, holding the coil in his right hand, backed up to the ridge and, paying out a little of the rope at a time, started down. His high-topped, lace-up boots scuffed and scratched at the uneven rock, occasionally breaking off a chunk and rattling it into the gully.

When he was a few feet from the gully floor, he jumped the rest, then removed the loop from around his waist and, glancing distastefully at the dead but still-spasming rattler, moved over to Yakima. He jerked his checked trousers up at the thighs and squatted down.

Yakima couldn't see the man's eyes, for his dusty spectacles mirrored salmon gold sunlight. "Can you move?"

Yakima's head throbbed and his vision

swam, but there was one overriding thought in his brain. "Faith . . . ?"

"I didn't see her. Did she make it out of the cabin?"

There was too much to explain. Yakima shook his head and grabbed the prospecting Easterner's arm. "Get me out of here."

"You sure nothing's broken, Yakima?"

He wasn't sure. The way he ached in every muscle and bone, he would have been surprised if something wasn't broken. His clothes were torn and bloody; he felt as though every inch of hide had been torn from his bones. He grabbed Harms's arm and climbed to his knees, breathing hard.

"That's a nasty notch in your forehead."

"Gotta get back . . . ," Yakima grunted, stretching his lips back from his teeth as, grinding his fingers into both of Harms's forearms, which had been thickened by two years of rock breaking, he hoisted himself to his feet.

"Easy."

Yakima grabbed the rope from the man's hand and turned to the opposite ridge where the mule stood, swishing its tail.

"Hold on," Harms said, "I'll help."

Yakima didn't wait for the help. He wasn't sure how much time had passed since the attack on the cabin, but he was relatively certain there was nothing he could do about it now. But he had to know what had happened after Wolf had dragged him out of the yard.

He picked up a rock and threw it at the mule. As the rock bounced off the animal's left hip, the mule gave an indignant snort and lurched forward. At the same time, Yakima grabbed the rope, and as the mule sort of skitter-hopped ahead and sideways, Yakima gripped the taut rope and quickly climbed the wall.

Ignoring the pain racking him, only vaguely aware that his buckskin shirt was hanging off his broad, muscular torso in torn strips, one sleeve completely gone, exposing his bleeding, dirt-encrusted arm, Yakima gained the ridge. Dizzy and feeling as though he'd vomit, he stumbled forward.

Getting his feet back under him, he steadied the mule, then threw the rope back down to Harms.

When the Easterner gained the ridge, Yakima grabbed the canteen off the mule's saddle, popped the cork, and took a long pull, drinking thirstily, then pouring some of the water across his face and over his head. The tepid water washed some of the dirt and blood from his face and somewhat braced him, but did nothing to slow the blacksmith hammer in his forehead.

"I was working my north hole when I saw the smoke," Harms said, breathing hard from the climb. He looked up at Yakima, face slack with worry. "Was it Apaches?"

Shaking his head, Yakima handed the canteen to Harms and, leaning against the mule, looked around to get his bearings. He felt as though he'd been hit with an Apache war hatchet and spun on a wagon wheel. When he finally got a handle on his location, he glanced north toward the yard.

Cedar-stippled knolls stood between him and the cabin a couple of hundred yards away. Gray smoke puffed above the pines.

He spat blood and water from his lips. "White men. One Mex. Didn't get a good look but I'd recognize 'em."

He grabbed the mule's reins and pulled himself onto the beast's broad back. "I'm gonna ride on back to the yard!" he grumbled as, leaving Harms staring incredulously after him, he ground his heels against the mule's ribs.

He felt as though the jolting, hammering ride, every stride a sledgehammer to his brain and aching muscles, was going to snuff his wick once more before he galloped around a low hill and brought the yard up in front of him. He drew the mule to a sudden stop and stared ahead in horror.

The cabin was little more than a mound of smoldering rubble. One of the side walls was only half standing, and the roof had collapsed. The sod of the roof must have doused most of the flames — only a few flares licked amidst the blackened logs — but smoke broiled skyward in massive, gray-black puffs, like that from an overheated locomotive.

Yakima gigged the horse toward the cabin, raking his eyes around. Spying a body lying in the soot-streaked dirt near the windmill, he swung down from the mule, trying to land more softly than he was able.

He stumbled over to where Kelly had fallen. The kid stared skyward through half-closed lids, his blue eyes glazed with death. The bullet hole in his forehead was jellied with dried blood. The sage and brown grass around him was crusted with blood, bone, and brains.

With a quivering hand, Yakima brushed Kelly's eyes closed. He rose slowly, groaning softly, and continued moving heavy-footed toward the cabin. He looked around, hoping he wouldn't find Faith in the same state as her brother.

After circling the cabin twice and scouring the brush and cedars at the base of

Bailey Creek, and finding nothing, he returned to the yard in front of the still-smoking cabin, pain-racked, fatigued, and dizzy, but hopeful that Faith was still alive.

The men had seemed about to take her when Yakima and Kelly had entered the hollow. They'd no doubt gone forward with their plan.

Who were they? And where were they taking her?

He had a nagging, miserable feeling that Bill Thornton had sent them, just as he'd sent Wit Bardoul.

Yakima looked at what remained of the cabin, and nausea nearly overwhelmed him, threatened to buckle his knees. He'd built the place over six long months of endless toil from the surrounding pines, and he'd filled his corral with the mustangs he was gentling for the surrounding Cavalry outposts.

Now his cabin was burned, his woman taken. Her brother, dead.

He looked around at the fresh horse tracks leading west from the yard. He discovered his Yellowboy lying in the dust, half concealed by a tumbleweed. He scooped it up and brushed dust from the barrel.

As he looked around again, his gaze settled upon his black stallion standing about a hundred yards out in the brush, reins dangling straight down from the bridle, the saddle hanging beneath the horse's belly. Wolf was peering toward the cabin, twitching his ears anxiously.

As he began tramping miserably along the trail toward the black, holding his rifle in one hand, Yakima saw Brody Harms's stocky, bespectacled figure moving toward him from the northwest, tramping over the sage-tufted hogbacks. Yakima strode through the ranch portal, and Harms headed toward him, scowling.

"Where do you think you're going?"

"The men who did this took Faith, Brody. I'm going after them."

Yakima continued walking toward Wolf, his vision blurred so that two blaze-faced stallions and part of a third stood staring at him warily. He could hear Harms walking up behind him.

"Yakima, I understand your eagerness to give chase," Harms said in his faint English accent. The son of a shipping magnate, he'd been born in Britain and had moved to Boston when he was ten. "But if you don't get that head wound wrapped, you'll bleed dry. You won't make it a mile."

Yakima set his jaws and approached the stallion, who turned his head and lifted his nose, sniffing the bloody trough carved across Yakima's temple. He grabbed the reins and the saddle horn, turned out the stirrup, and, sucking a deep breath, raised his leg.

He missed the stirrup, dropped his Winchester. Grabbing the apple with both hands, he sagged against the horse, gritting his teeth, plundering his core for strength. He felt blood dribbling wetly down the side of his face and neck.

Harms stepped up beside him, bending to retrieve the Yellowboy. "You can't even climb into the saddle. Besides, the horse needs tending, too. Looks like he took some lead himself."

Yakima pushed away from Wolf and ran his gaze across the animal's sleek black hide. There were several nasty gashes across his hip and neck, and an especially deep one across his left wither.

Wolf had no serious wounds, but the cards were stacked against Yakima. He'd have to wait until at least tomorrow to start trailing Faith.

He heaved a long sigh and stared off in the direction the riders had taken her. Then he swung around and began leading Wolf toward the stallion's corral. Harms walked beside him in pensive silence, the Easterner's mule calmly grazing off the trail's left side.

Yakima paused beside Kelly's body. "Will you bury the kid for me?"

"Of course," Harms said. "After I tend you."

He took the reins out of Yakima's hand. "You go on into the stable and lie down. I'll put Wolf away and scrounge up some water and bandages. I have a whiskey bottle in my saddlebags."

Yakima let the man take the reins. He grabbed his rifle. With one more glance at Kelly lying dead near the corral post, he spat blood from his lips and continued forward past the empty corrals, then turned and headed for the stable.

His moccasined feet were growing heavy as iron wheel hubs.

CHAPTER 9

Faith half dozed in the saddle she was tied to, her leather-bound wrists wrapped around the saddle horn of the bay mare the men had taken from the corral at the ranch.

Since she'd been captured by the bounty hunters four hours ago, she'd gone from heart-aching misery and uncontrolled sobbing to raw, blue fury and back again. The image of her brother lying piled up against the stock tank with half his brains blown out would not leave her. Nor would the memory of Yakima being shot out of his saddle and dragged westward across the brushy knobs.

Kelly was dead. Yakima was probably dead, too, already being gnawed on by wolves or coyotes. Doubtless, the cabin was no more than gray ashes.

A fresh, raw wave of sorrow and horror overcame her once more, and she bowed her head, cursing and squeezing her eyes closed against the tears rolling down her cheeks. She tried to keep her sobs to herself, stubbornly refusing to let these cold-blooded killers see that they had broken her.

She opened her eyes when the mare stopped. A few yards ahead of her, the mare's reins in his hand, the man called Temple had halted his own horse on the lip of a shallow ravine, and turned to regard the other men behind Faith.

"We'll stop here for the night. Chulo, you and Kooch go down and check it out."

As the two men broke off from the group, separating as they descended the cut, Faith saw Temple regarding her with furrowed brows. "Shut up. I don't wanna hear no more of that."

Faith was about to ask him what he'd meant, but stopped. She must have been sobbing more loudly than she'd thought.

"This is Apache country," Temple said in his low, raspy voice. "An Apache can hear a pet mouse scratchin' around in your saddle-bags."

Faith hardened her jaw and narrowed her eyes. Her rage at the man, the others, and the man who'd hired him — Bill Thornton — was monumental. The words she was able to find in her grief-tortured mind sounded childish and feeble in comparison.

"I don't have any pet mice scratchin' around in my saddlebags, you son of a bitch."

"No, but that's what you sound like, carryin' on. What's done is done."

"You killed my brother. My man."

"Stow it."

Faith set her jaws. Sitting the saddle and staring at the lead bounty hunter's back, she felt tears of grief and horror dribble down her cheeks.

Temple had turned to stare into the ravine in which the scouts had disappeared. A hundred yards beyond the ravine, a high sandstone dike glowed copper as the molten orb of the sun sank quickly behind the dark, western ridges. Far off, a hawk screeched like the high-pitched rake of an un-oiled hinge — a lonely, seemingly bodiless sound.

"If you let me go, I'll pay you as much as Thornton has."

She stopped when the outlaw leader turned his head toward her sharply. Something inside her recoiled when he unexpectedly smiled, his gray eyes reflecting the waning light. "Shut up or I'll slap ya silly."

One of the scouts called up from the draw, "Nothin' down here but sand and snakeskins, Temple."

The lead bounty hunter glanced at the others and canted his head forward. He yanked on the reins of Faith's mount and raked his spurs against his gelding's flanks; the dun gave an indignant jerk as it started down the brushy slope.

They were in the sandy-bottomed draw, which boasted a high northern bank, in less than a minute. Temple pulled up to where Kooch Manley and Chulo Garza were unsaddling their horses in a deep bend. Both men turned to look at Faith.

"Hey, Temple," the middle-aged Manley said, grinning conspiratorially at the Mexican as he tossed his saddlebags down. "How 'bout I give you five dollars of my bounty money for a few hours with the lady?"

Temple swung down from his saddle. Slipping a knife from a shoulder sheath beneath his coat, he sauntered back to Faith with a weary sigh. "I told you," he grumbled. "I ain't her pimp, and she ain't for sale, fellas. Let's let that be the end of it, all right?"

The two men chuckled. The blond bulldog, whose name was Frank Miller, rode up beside Faith and regarded Temple angrily. "Let me get this straight. We gotta ride all the way back to Colorado" — he threw an arm out toward Faith — *"lookin'* at that, and that's *all?* Just *lookin'?"*

Temple extended the knife toward Faith, his mouth corners lifting as his eyes traveled slowly up her buckskin coat. " 'Jesus was led up of the Spirit into the wilderness to be tempted of the devil.' "

"Yeah, well, we ain't Jesus," said the goat-bearded kid, Benny Freeze. "We're just men who haven't dipped our wicks in a month of Sundays!"

"You got that right, Benny," Miller laughed. "We are most certainly in the wilderness and she . . . boy, don't she look like a spirit, though?"

The others laughed while Temple cut the rawhide tying Faith's boots to her stirrups, then pulled her down out of the saddle. He led her away from the horse and shoved her brusquely down against the arroyo's shaded northwest wall. He tied two of the shorter rawhide strips together and used it to tie her ankles about five inches apart.

"I'll leave your hands free," he said, straightening and putting a hand to the small of his creaking back. "Unless you try anything foxy. Understand?"

Faith glowered up at him. The other men were leading their horses down the arroyo where Garza had found some grama grass. Faith's heart fluttered with freshly stoked anger and bitter memories as she said, "What does Thornton intend to do with me? Beat me? Carve me up? *Shoot* me?"

Temple stared down at her, lifting his hat and running a hand through his long, thin hair. "I don't know what he intends. But it is my intention to see that you're delivered safe and sound, so that your former employer — against whom it seems your transgressions are grave — may do to you as he wishes." Temple winked. "I'm just a businessman. I've agreed to do a job, and I'm gonna see it through."

He turned and began to walk toward his horse.

"Wait," Faith said on a sudden impulse.

Temple glanced back at her.

"Cut me loose." She glanced at the rawhide tying her ankles together and funneled as much fake sincerity into her voice as she could. "I'll gather wood."

"Like hell you will."

"Please. Let me do something. I've been sitting on that horse for the past four hours. I need to move around, get my blood circulating." Faith tipped her hat brim against the harsh, last rays of the sun, and frowned at the tattooed, gray-eyed man arching a brow at her. "If I tried to run, how far could I get? You'd either run me down, or Apaches would. And there's border bandits galore. I doubt they'd be as respectful as you, to your credit, have been so far. . . ."

The place was honeycombed with hostiles of every stripe. But the Eastern gold seeker — Brody Harms — who'd become a close friend of Faith, Yakima, and Kelly, had a cabin near Buzzard Butte. If she could make it to Harms's cabin, he'd help her get back to the ranch.

She was still clinging to the slender hope that, while Kelly was dead, Yakima was not. Temple and the others had scoured the brush for him but had been unable to find him.

Temple stared at her, slitting a pensive eye at her, thinking it over. Her pulse throbbed. She might not be able to outrun these men, but if she could hide until after dark, she'd try to find her way to Buzzard Butte under cover of darkness.

"Why not?" Temple reached into his coat for a wide bowie knife. "Never been against a woman earnin' her keep. You can cook, too, once you get a fire goin'."

"Sure," Faith said as the man squatted at her feet and slid the razor-edged blade across the leather, which gave instantly.

He stood and returned the knife to its sheath. "Don't disappoint me now, hear?"

Temple turned and began walking toward his horse and the other men, who were rubbing down their own mounts while smoking and talking in hushed tones. Kooch Manley had popped the cork on a bottle and was passing it around. As Temple approached the group, Miller pointed the bottle toward Faith, who had gained her feet and was strolling ever so slowly, with painstaking casualness, westward along the arroyo.

"Hey, where's she goin'?"

"Fetchin' firewood," Temple said, reaching under his horse to unbuckle the latigo.

Manley cursed. "You think that's a good idea?"

"If she tried to make like the wind," said Miller, who sat down on his saddle to build a smoke, "I'd be happy to run her down. Maybe I could sneak one in before Temple laid into us with his Jesus whip!"

Faith had been glancing over her shoulder at the men as she moved nonchalantly down the arroyo. Spying a piece of driftwood in the corner of her eye, she moved over to pick it up, then continued forward, hearing the men talking behind her, feeling their eyes on her back. She picked up two more sun-bleached branches before she glanced again over her shoulder.

The men were out of sight around a bend.

Her heart instantly began racing, her brain swirling as she looked around and tried to clarify her thoughts. She had to get as far away as possible, find a notch cave or a snag of brush or boulders — any hiding place at all — and hope like hell they didn't find her.

Faith dropped the wood and pushed into a jog down the sandy-bottomed canyon, continuing to glance over her shoulder to make sure she wasn't being followed. The men's sounds dwindled behind her — their occasional laughter and the clatter of tack. Then the sounds disappeared and she could hear only her own breathing, her own foot thuds, and the rustle of the branches on the arroyo's right bank.

The dull hoot of an owl made her stop suddenly with a startled gasp.

Pressing a hand to her chest as if to quell her leaping heart, she continued forward. Ahead, the arroyo branched. She took the left fork, glancing back to see her boot prints in the flood-scalloped sand and gravel. Suddenly, she lurched right onto a boulder, leaped from that boulder to another, then to the top of the bank, pulling herself up with gnarled mesquite roots, trying to leave as little sign as possible.

The high sandstone ridge, purpling now as the sun sank from view, quartered off to her right as she ran through the chaparral ten minutes later, hot blood racing through her veins, heart pounding. Anxiety, hope, and desperation churned a toxic, energizing elixir that fairly lifted her off her feet.

Every step took her that much farther from the cutthroats. Every step took her that much closer to Brody Harms's cabin.

She slowed her pace to look behind. Nothing but rocks, rotting mesquite branches, and creosote spreading their slender arms toward the dark green sky. A small rabbit hunkered down in the lee of an arrow-shaped boulder, pressing its ears to its head, trying to make itself look like a stone.

Nothing moved back there. Not even the breeze. No sounds whatever. In the northwest, the top of the sandstone ridge glowed like molten iron, the light diminishing as Faith watched, pricking her ears to listen for footsteps or the drumming of hooves.

The silence chilled her. Surely by now they knew she'd run. What were they doing?

Should she continue running or hole up until after good dark?

A kangaroo rat chittered nearby. Faith sucked a sharp, startled breath, then turned to continue jogging.

Her right boot clipped a deadfall log, and she went down hard on her chest, her breath hammered out of her lungs in a single, loud grunt. She winced as gravel and goatheads bit into her hands and her chin.

A spine-tingling rattle sounded, like the prolonged cocking of a gun hammer. She looked ahead and right.

A diamondback rattler lay under an up-jutting branch of another deadfall log. Its body was coiled like an expertly wound lariat, its head hovering six inches above the ground, its diamond-shaped eyes regarding Faith with cold malevolence. The rattles rose and fell slightly, quivering, the sound ominously changing pitch.

Muscles drawn taut as fence wire, Faith pushed off her right hand slowly, tilting her body away from the snake.

"Easy," she breathed.

She drew a knee up and sideways, then the other.

The snake watched her, sliding its flat head slowly toward her, its tongue slithering in and out of its mouth.

"Easy . . ."

Keeping her eyes on the snake as if to hold it with her stare, Faith crawled back out of striking distance. She rose slowly, took one slow step forward, then lurched into another run.

She'd taken only two steps, still looking

behind at the snake, before she smashed headlong into a man in her path. With a startled cry, she fell back and hit the dirt and gravel on her butt, staring up in horror at the man grinning down at her through a thick gray-black beard. The man's brown left eye sparked lustily while the other, white as fresh-whipped cream, glowed wickedly as though lit from within.

He chuckled, throwing his sombrero-clad head back on his shoulders. "Senorita!"

She tried to scuttle back on her butt, but he crouched and grabbed her wrists in his hands, raking his eyes across her body. More laughter rose behind him, and she glanced up to see two more Mexicans — one sitting on a rock with a rifle between his knees, another standing nearby and holding a revolver straight down by his side. Saddles and camping gear were strewn around them, but there was no fire.

Faith tried to jerk her wrists free of the big Mexican's gloved, viselike grip.

"*Jesus* has blessed us this night, amigos!" he whooped.

He lowered his head toward Faith's, pooching out his lips. A rifle barked to Faith's left, and the man's head jerked in the opposite direction. He grunted and stumbled backward, his hands still wrapped firmly around Faith's wrists and pulling her back as he sagged. Blood spewed from a gaping hole in his left temple.

The Mexican hit the ground on his back, and Faith fell facedown on his chest with an anguished groan, the hide-wrapped handle of a knife sheathed under his arm raking her cheek.

"Mierda!" one of the other banditos shouted.

A rifle barked six times in quick succession, each blast followed by the angry rasp of a cocking lever.

Faith buried her face in the chest of the bandito quivering beneath her. Ahead, the other two men wailed and screamed, boots thudding. But as the last rifle report ceased echoing across the still, twilit desert, the men fell silent.

The salty aroma of cordite thick in her nostrils, Faith lifted her head from the bandito's unmoving chest and glanced to her left.

Lowry Temple stood atop the knoll, crouched over the smoking Winchester angled slightly down from his right hip. Faith followed the man's gaze to where the other two banditos lay sprawled around their gear, one on his side and bleeding from several wounds in his chest, the other on his back, spread-eagled, as though he'd been staked out by Apaches.

Blood gushed from his ruined eye sockets.

She looked at the man she'd fallen on. He was still shaking slightly. Blood continued spewing from the side of his head though not as energetically as a second ago. His wide-open eyes stared at the darkening sky beyond Faith.

Faith made a sour expression. Her stomach contracted against the stench of death and powder smoke. She pushed away from the dead Mexican and sat back on her rump, drawing her knees to her chest.

The rifle reports still echoed in her head. As her eyes found Temple grinning down at her, she convulsed with a sob.

Temple off-cocked his Winchester's hammer and set the gun on his shoulder. "Seen those three doggin' us a couple hours ago." He spat a tobacco quid onto a rock. "Figured you'd flush 'em out for me. Didn't know you were gonna lead me right into their camp!"

Faith said nothing. Tears dribbled down her cheeks as she stared through the wafting smoke at the dead men. Temple rolled his chaw around in his mouth and spat another long quid onto the chest of the still Mexican sprawled in front of Faith.

"Come on," Temple called. "You was gonna fetch some wood, remember?"

CHAPTER 10

"Faith!"

Yakima's own shout awakened him, and he sat bolt upright, instantly biting his lip as a dull lance blade impaled his skull, dropping a bright red veil of pain across his eyes.

Somewhere to his left a cot creaked and a voice rasped, "What is it?"

Then it all came back to Yakima in a flood of barbed memories pummeling his aching brain. As he stared through the darkness at the cracks in the stable door etched with misty, predawn light, he sucked a deep, weary breath.

"Shit."

In the dream, Faith had been falling away from him into a deep, black pit as wide as the hell that the priests in a Denver boarding school had once told him about, assuring him that if he didn't accept their ways, he himself would tumble into that black, fire-bottomed pit of eternal damnation.

But it was Faith he still saw now — her strong, clean-lined face with its dimpled chin and frank blue eyes fading quickly from his view. Down, down, down, and away from him, swallowed by thick, hot, tarlike blackness.

"Well, that's one way to wake up," Brody Harms sighed. "Dream?"

Yakima grunted, dropped his feet to the chill, hay-flecked floor, and raked his hands across his face. "It's coming onto dawn. I'll build up the fire."

He was reluctant to take the time for breakfast, but he'd lost blood and needed to regain his strength. Last night, he'd donned longhandles from the wooden locker he kept in the stable, filled with spare duds. Now he ransacked the locker again for a pair of denims, a patched buckskin shirt, and an old, ratty jaguar coat. He found a spare cartridge belt, filled it with .44 shells from a box at the bottom of the locker, and wrapped it around his waist so that it overlapped his pistol belt.

He had a feeling he was going to need all the ammo he could get his hands on.

When he'd made sure his stag-butted .44 was loaded, he pulled on his moccasin boots and hat and headed outside. He kicked down the ashes from last night's cook fire just outside the stable door, and tossed kindling into the ring.

A few minutes later, the fire was crackling in the chill dawn, and he and Brody Harms hunkered down around it, eating the salt pork and beans that Harms had carried in his saddlebags, and washing the food down with hot, black coffee.

"I'll be pullin' out," Yakima said, tossing his dregs into the fire. "Much obliged for the doctorin', Brody."

Harms held his plate up close to his mustached face, shoveling the last bite of pork and beans into his mouth. "I'm going with you. Got most of my camping gear in my saddlebags. I'm down to one mule — that mad-eyed devil yonder." Chewing, he glanced at Yakima. "Don't have a lot of ammo, though."

"I can't ask you to come. I don't even know who those bastards are or where they're headed. Besides, it's my woman they have."

"Faith's my friend." Harms scrubbed his plate with a handful of fire ash and dust. "Kelly was my friend. And you're my friend, too."

He dropped his plate into his saddlebags, then reached over for Yakima's. "Understand?"

Yakima nodded, stood, and kicked dirt on the fire. "I've got ammo. We won't need much if we wait till we see their eyes. I don't intend on giving them a chance. No chance at all. They killed Kelly and took Faith, and they're going to die for that."

Adjusting his possibles in his saddle pouches, Harms looked up at Yakima standing over him, the half-breed's large red fists balled at his sides. Harms felt himself wince at the simmering, savage rage he saw in Yakima's keen green eyes — the German eyes he'd inherited from his father and which were a startling contrast to his otherwise dark, primitive Indian features.

The Easterner nodded. He felt a fleeting apprehension at what lay ahead, knowing it would be a hard trail with a bloody end.

He stood and threw his saddlebags over a shoulder, and they moved over to Wolf and the mule, both standing saddled outside Wolf's corral, looking fresh and ready to go.

Yakima had tried not to look at the cabin, but now, as the pale dawn thickened, with buttery sunlight showing behind Bailey Peak, he turned his eyes to the burned-out hulk. Only a few charred logs remained, enclosing drifts of snow-like ash.

"You'll get her back, Yakima."

Yakima turned to Harms sitting his mule

beside him, frowning behind his dusty spectacles.

"You'll get her back, and the two of you will rebuild your place."

Yakima glanced once more at the cabin. Kelly's grave flanked it on a low knoll, the rock-covered mound marked by a crude cross that Harms had fashioned from pine branches and rawhide last night before they'd both turned in.

Yakima swung into the saddle and reined Wolf westward across the yard and out the ranch portal. He and Harms nudged their mounts into lopes along the trail in which the cutthroats' tracks were still etched like demonic hieroglyphics showing the way to hell.

The kidnappers' trail wasn't hard to follow. Riding with bold confidence that no one would follow them, believing most likely that Yakima's head wound or the dragging or both had been fatal, they did nothing to cover their tracks as they headed straight west of the ranch.

The two trackers left the old two-track prospector's trail near Hermit Butte and angled north through a broad valley bordered in the west and east by vast, bizarrely sculpted sandstone formations.

Straight north lay the hazy, flat-topped form of Black Mesa, with the Sierra Mogollons quartering off to the northwest, resembling storm clouds from this distance of a hundred miles or more, with lower, barren, dun-colored ranges rumpling up in front of them.

Yakima didn't have to push Wolf to make good time that morning. The black mustang seemed to sense his rider's urgency and determination, and kept up its pace without prodding.

Harms's mule was another matter. More accustomed to pulling a buckboard tool wagon and standing for long hours in the shaded lee of an escarpment while its owner ravaged a vein with pick and shovel, the owl-eyed beast required near-constant spurring. It could keep up with Wolf when it wanted to, but mostly it lagged.

Harms cursed the beast and batted its ribs with his heels. The mule chugged and blew and, occasionally, hee-hawed and bucked, tail in the air.

Late morning, Yakima halted Wolf on a rocky hill and peered into the canyon on his right. The cut ran along the base of a pine-carpeted slope spotted with slide rock and gray deadfall. At a wide part of the canyon, the broom-tail bronc stood, lapping water contentedly from a run-out spring bubbling around mossy stones. Up-canyon a ways, Yakima's mares and foals milled — a remuda of twenty valuable horses — cropping needle grass and bluestem while lazily swishing their tails.

The bronc lifted its head slightly, its entire body quivering, its lips stretching back from its teeth. The mustang's whinny sounded a half second later — a bugling cry of victory.

Wolf answered, bobbing his head angrily.

Yakima scowled down at the mustang and the harem he'd won at last. "Take care of those girls," the half-breed growled. "I'll be back for 'em."

The bugling cry sounded again, frightening the foals up-canyon, who jerked and skitter-hopped away from their mothers.

"I wonder what he just called you," Harms said, heeling the disgruntled mule up the bluff behind Yakima.

"Nothing I haven't called him, I reckon," the half-breed said, clucking Wolf on down the bluff's other side.

At noon they followed the kidnappers' tracks into a meandering cut and drew rein before a fire ring heaped with gray ashes and three charred tins with twisted, dangling lids. A few unused pine branches lay beside the ring.

Around lay the prints of the kidnappers' horses, all of which Yakima had memorized, and near the arroyo's north wall he saw the indentation of Faith's boots — smaller than the others and marked in the heel with a small, rearing bronc, which was the signature of the man who'd made them in Saber Creek.

Yakima swung down from Wolf, crouched over the fire ring, removed his right glove, and sifted the ashes through his fingers. "They pulled out early."

While Harms dismounted and slopped water into his hat for the beast, Yakima walked around, following the cutthroats' trail up a notch in the northern wall, about forty yards away from the fire ring. He climbed the wall and kicked around the hoof-pocked caliche, then wandered along the ridge back toward Harms, who'd rolled a cigarette and stood smoking it bareheaded, his thick, sweat-damp brown hair showing the mark of his hat, which was on the ground in front of the mule. He looked up the ridge at Yakima, letting smoke dribble out from between his lips.

"You have any idea where they're headed?"

The half-breed kicked a stone in frustration. "North. That's all I know. They seem bound and determined to get somewhere . . . but where, and for what reason, I got no idea. Unless . . ."

Yakima let his voice trail off. He'd been wondering if the men had been sent by Thornton, but he couldn't imagine the roadhouse manager holding a grudge that long. Two years had passed since Faith had shot him, and he must have realized by now that he'd had it coming.

Yakima had worried all morning that he'd find Faith dead along the trail. He was infinitely relieved that he hadn't, that the men who'd grabbed her obviously wanted her for more than their goatish pleasure.

But if they'd been sent by Thornton, they no doubt intended to take her to Colorado Territory, which meant the trail could be long and hard. He had to catch up to them before their sign gave out — before they decided to start covering their tracks, or before a rain- or windstorm erased it.

They were moving fast. Yakima figured he might have gained an hour on them, but he wouldn't be able to continue gaining on them with Harms's mule holding him back. He'd considered sending the Easterner back to his diggings, but if he was going to get Faith back, he'd need all the help he could get.

Yakima wandered farther north from the ridge and stopped. His eyes raked the ground around the kidnappers' tightly grouped hoofprints. He strode a few paces farther forward, then stopped again and squinted down at the tracks moving onto the cutthroats' trail from the east.

He removed his glove again and traced the outline of one of the unshod hooves with his fingertips. The tracks were several hours fresher than those of the kidnappers'. He'd spied the same tracks a few miles back, and he'd been carrying a knife blade of dread in his belly ever since.

His expression must have betrayed his concern, because after he'd scuttled down the ridge and into the arroyo, Harms removed his quirley from between his lips and cocked his head at him curiously. "What's wrong?"

"Injuns on their trail." Yakima grabbed Wolf's dangling reins. "Four, looks like. Coyoteros, probably."

"Shit."

"Depending on how you look at it," Yakima said as he swung up onto the stallion's back, "it ain't all bad."

"Indians aren't bad?" Scowling, Harms quickly field-stripped his quirley, then mounted the skitter-stepping mule, which

131

brayed belligerently, flicking its long ears. "Did that bullet crease your brain as well as your skull?"

"Nothin' bad about gettin' our hands on extra horses." Yakima glanced at Harms. "If you and I both had a couple Indian ponies, we'd overtake that gang before sundown!"

With that, he gigged Wolf up-canyon in a fury of pounding hooves and lifting dust.

"What in the name of King George are you talking about?" Harms called behind him, heeling the mule forward. "No," he add darkly, shaking his head. "Don't think I wanna know."

CHAPTER 11

"Jumpin' Jehosophat!" Brody Harms whispered. "You're a raving lunatic — you know that?"

"Been called such, time or two."

"You're going to steal horses from *Apaches?*"

"Why not? They've done it to me. Seems only fair I should return the favor."

They were hunkered down in the rocks and shrubs along a high, sloping mountain wall. Yakima was staring through his field glasses, adjusting the focus until he'd clarified the tendril of smoke rising from a nest of rocks about a hundred and fifty yards downslope and southwest of his and Harms's position. The smoke was a thin gray wisp among the rocks, boulders, and cacti behind it.

Yakima and Harms had followed the cutthroats and the four unshod horses trailing them until an hour ago, when the unshod prints had suddenly veered from those of the shod horses, climbing a rocky slope toward a bald ridge. Hiding their own mounts in a secluded hollow, Yakima and Harms had shucked their rifles and climbed the ridge, swinging wide of the Indians' trail.

Yakima intended to recon the Apache camp and then, depending on where the bivouac was located and how good a view the Indians had of the surrounding terrain, devise a way to slip into the bivouac and make off with the Apaches' mustangs.

The half-breed's intention was not only to acquire a couple of Indian ponies for Harms, but to secure an extra one for himself. With two mounts apiece, they could ride twice as fast and overtake the cut-throats who'd kidnapped Faith in half the time it would take them with only Wolf and Harms's increasingly problematic mule.

"Indeed, it does *sound* fair," Harms growled, having removed his spectacles to rub the dust around with his gloved fingers. "But I thought our intention was to get your wife back, not get ourselves killed in the process."

"You're right." Yakima turned to the stocky, sunburned Easterner hunkered down beside him. "This wasn't part of the bargain. I'm gonna need an extra horse, but there's no reason why you should risk your hide. You and your mule head home."

Frowning, holding his bowler hat in his thick hands, Harms opened his mouth to speak, but Yakima cut him off with "There's no dishonor in being smart."

Harms looked at him pensively for a stretched second, then turned onto his back, looking around at the penny-colored rocks humping out of the brush around them. "I ever tell you why I came out here?"

"You said somethin' about not getting along with your family."

"That was part of it. I've always been the black sheep in the Harms household, favoring art and music more than the company my father owns. Then, there was this girl I married. I'd loved her since I was eight years old. Looked a lot like Faith. Redefined female beauty."

With the back of his hand, he brushed dust from his frayed hat brim. "I came home from my father's office early one day, and found her doing the mattress dance with a young man she and I had gone to school with. A kid from the wrong side of the tracks, you might say. Turned out she'd always been in love with *him*, just as I'd always been in love with *her*. She'd married me because my father convinced her it

135

would be in the best interest of her and her family."

Yakima shook his head. "I'm sorry, Brody, but what's this got to do with stealing Apache horses?"

"The next day, I packed a bag and a bedroll, left a note on my father's desk, and jumped the train west. I rode the rails aimlessly for nigh on a month. Didn't know what I was going to do until, somewhere around Santa Fe, I threw in with some prospectors and decided to head out after my own El Dorado.

"Now I live alone in a couple of cramped cabins in the middle of this godforsaken desert, drawing pictures of rocks and cactus by lamplight at night, and hammering rocks by day." Harms turned to Yakima sharply, squinting an eye behind his dusty spectacles. "What you and Faith have is a rare thing. I'd like to help you hold on to it." He took a deep breath. "Now, let's show those Apaches how to steal horses."

Yakima held his friend's wry gaze for a moment, then turned to give the Apache encampment another gander. After a minute, he held the glasses out to Harms and said softly, "Take a good look downslope."

Harms doffed his bowler, crawled over to

where Yakima had been lying between two large boulders, and leaned forward on his elbows, aiming the field glasses between the rocks.

After a minute, he lowered the glasses and glanced over his shoulder at Yakima. "Got it."

"Crab down the other side of this slope. Crawl, I'm sayin'. Belly down against the dirt. At the bottom of the slope, jog up the next one but do it *quietly.* You see that little snag of brick-colored rocks spiking up atop the hill, just left of the barrel cactus?"

Harms turned to gaze through the glasses once more. "Yeah."

"Stop right there. The Indians should be right below you — maybe twenty, thirty yards down the hill."

"You want me to fling some lead?"

"No. I want you to fling a rock." Yakima picked up his Yellowboy, rubbed dust from the gold-chased receiver into which two wolves fighting a grizzly had been etched. "But do it gentle-like, like it just rolled down the bank."

"Like a mouse nudged it."

"You got it."

Yakima scuttled backward down the rise, then rose and shouldered the rifle. He stared down the slope toward the trail at the valley's bottom — a flat-bottomed bowl bristling with creosote, barrel cactus, saguaro, and mesquite thickets surrounded by countless camelbacks and dinosaur spines of sandstone. Plenty of cover, but there was no such thing as adequate cover when you were shadowing Apaches.

"Give me a half hour to get around behind them," Yakima said. "Then drop the rock."

"Just like a mouse nudged it."

Yakima jogged down the slope, heading off in the opposite direction of the Coyoteros before swinging south. He made a broad, slow sweep across the bowl of bristling chaparral, pausing often to look around, making sure he hadn't been spotted or that the Apaches weren't breaking camp and heading toward him.

When he figured he was due west of the Apache camp, he began moving forward, setting each moccasin boot down carefully, looking around for the Coyotero horses. An Apache mustang's senses were as keen as a jaguar's; if they winded him, they'd give him away. He doubted the braves would have picketed their mounts very far from their day camp, which meant Yakima probably wouldn't be able to lead them off without a fight.

A feather of aromatic smoke touched his

nostrils, and his mouth watered as he identi-fied the warm tang of roasting javelina. So that's why the braves had stopped early. They'd shot a wild pig.

The smell of the roasting meat grew stronger as he meandered among the rocks and cholla. Hearing a soft snort, he jerked a look into a nest of rocks and cedars ahead and right. A horse with a braided green and white halter peered at him from around a boulder. Yakima gritted his teeth as the horse widened its eyes, laid its ears back, and lifted a shrill whinny so loud that Yakima's battered head began throbbing anew.

A shadow flicked across the face of the boulder, and, squeezing the Yellowboy in his gloved hands, Yakima wheeled. A brickred visage clad in dun deerskin and a red bandanna dove toward him off a flat-topped boulder, holding a feathered war hatchet in his right hand, and a bloody butcher knife in his left.

Yakima lifted the Winchester's barrel and roared off a shot. The Indian grunted as the slug tore through his belly in midair, blow-ing dust from his deerskin tunic but doing nothing to check the Indian's dive.

Yakima dropped the rifle as the brave continued flying toward him, and wrapped his left hand around the brave's right wrist, his right hand around the brave's left, stopping the plunge of both weapons only a few inches from his head. The brave's momentum threw him straight back, and he hit the ground hard, the brave wailing shrilly while twisting and writhing and pressing the hatchet and knife toward Yakima's throat.

Gripping the brave's wrists, Yakima drove the weakening younker to his left, surprised to find no ground there. His stomach whipped toward his throat as, still clinging to each other and writhing savagely, he and the brave dropped straight down through empty air.

Beneath Yakima, still gripping the knife and the hatchet, the brave wailed and looked around, coffee-colored eyes wide with shock and rage, the wind from their plunge lifting his coarse black hair from his shoulders.

The brave's back smacked the rocks and gravel ten feet beneath the ledge, dust puffing around him. Yakima fell on top of him, pushing the knife blade back against the brave's own neck. He carved a short but deep red gash over the Indian's Adam's apple just before gravity grabbed them once more and flung them down a steep, talus-strewn slope.

As they rolled together over rocks and sage tufts, branches snapping and rocks clattering, Yakima felt the tension leave the brave's limbs. The war hatchet dropped from his right hand, and Yakima flung the younker away from him as he tried in vain to check his roll.

An upthrust of rock moved up quickly from downslope to smack him hard about the chest and shoulders, checking his tumble and evoking a sharp grunt as it smashed the air from his lungs.

Piled up at the base of the rock, Yakima rolled onto his back and clutched at his throbbing, bandaged head with both hands. Fast foot beats and rasping breaths rose on his left. He turned his aching head to peer upslope.

Two more braves ran toward him, leaping like panthers and yapping like coyotes. They both held revolvers and knives and their dark eyes sparkled in the sunlight, teeth showing between spread lips — eager for the slow torture and kill.

Yakima slapped leather, snaked his cocked revolver across his belly, and fired. The brave on the left shrieked as the slug punched through his upper right chest. He stumbled, fell, and rolled.

The other Indian stopped suddenly with

an enraged yowl. Cocking his octagonal-barreled Colt Navy, he raised the revolver and fired.

The slug barked into the rock above Yakima's right shoulder, spraying dust and stone shards. Yakima drew a bead on the brave as the Apache spread his feet to steady his own aim.

Yakima traded shots with the brave, the brave's slug crashing into the talus in front of Yakima as the half-breed's own slug drilled the brave through his heart.

A third shot barked from above.

As the brave stumbled back up the slope with the force of Yakima's bullet, his head exploded, spewing blood and brains downslope to his right.

The brave's head jerked sharply, twisting the lifeless body and throwing the man's limbs akimbo. The Coyotero hit the slope with a clattering thud and rolled like a windblown sack.

Yakima looked upslope. Brody Harms knelt on one knee, aiming his Spencer repeater at the two dead Apaches, smoke from his shot still puffing in the still air around his bowler-hatted head. A figure rose behind him, the Apache's stocky, broad-shouldered frame silhouetted against the rocky hill behind him.

As the Apache lifted a spear for a killing stab, Yakima's heart raced, and he shouted, *"Look out, Brody!"*

Harms swung around quickly, half rising, and slammed his rifle against the spear, sending it clattering onto the rocks.

Yakima's eyes blurred slightly. They didn't focus again until he saw Harms and the Indian rolling together down a lower bank than the one from which Yakima and his own Apache had tumbled. Harms and the Indian rolled together like a couple of fighting bears, both snarling, grunting, punching, and kicking.

Yakima heaved himself to his feet, cocked his Colt, and stumbled across the slope as Harms stopped rolling and gave the Apache a savage kick. The Apache screamed as he rose off his feet and hit the ground on his back.

The brave turned a fluid backward somersault and came up facing Harms, spitting grit and crouching, his seamed, leathery face a mask of animal fury.

Yakima raised the Colt but before he could fire, Harms bolted toward the Indian, squared his shoulders, spread his legs, and raised his fists, the backs of his hands facing the Apache as though he were holding his knuckles up for inspection.

"Brody, get away!" Yakima shouted, holding the shot.

Harms and the Indian faced each other, the Indian's uncertain eyes betraying his befuddlement at the white man's exotic stance. Lips pursed and jaws jutting, arms hooked in front of him like question marks, his big hands clenched into bright red fists, Harms saw his opening.

The Easterner threw his fists straight forward and up, hitting the Apache square in the face — three solid smacks in quick succession. The Indian's head bobbed up and down. He stumbled backward, eyes snapping wide with exasperation, blood glistening on his cut lips.

He gave a wild mew, his features stretched with incredulity, then reached for a large knife sashed on his waist. He hadn't gotten a hand on the blade's horn handle before Harms lunged once more. Brody faked a jab with his left fist, then laid two slashing rights in the middle of the Coyotero's broad, flat face.

As the Apache stumbled back toward a fir tree, throwing his arms out for balance, Yakima, who stood in skeptical amazement, holding his revolver barrel up in his right hand, saw that the brave's nose had been smashed flat against his face.

Tomato red blood splashed in all directions across his cheeks.

The brave cupped his ruined nose in his hands, giving a nasal yowl. Harms grabbed his own bowie knife from his belt, stepped fleetly forward, and buried the wide blade hilt-deep in the Apache's belly.

The brave screamed and fell back against the tree, crouching over the knife that Harms angled up toward the heart, his face, minus its glasses, stretched with fury.

He pulled the blade out quickly. Blood gushed from the Indian's middle like wine from a bladder flask.

Harms stepped back as the Apache dropped to his knees, crumpling as though all his bones had turned to putty. He farted loudly, jerked a couple of times, and lay still.

Yakima stared at the dead Indian, still not quite believing his eyes, then slowly depressed his Colt's hammer. Just as slowly, he lowered the gun to his side.

He looked at Harms, who stood in the fir's shade, breathing heavily, blood banding off his knife blade as he, too, stared down at the dead Apache.

Yakima gazed at his Eastern friend, incredulity carving deep lines in his russet forehead. "Where in the hell did you learn to fight like that?"

"West Point," the Easterner said. He shot Yakima a wry grin. He'd lost his hat and his glasses, and sweat and dust streaked his broad, handsome face with its expressive brown eyes set under heavy brows. His hair, hacked unevenly, was caked with dust and pine needles. "Before they kicked me out for daydreaming."

Harms sighed as he leaned forward to clean his knife on the back of the Indian's calico shirt.

"Well, then," he said, as Yakima continued staring at him in shocked silence. "Since we went to all this work to fetch their horses, I reckon we'd better fetch them and get after your woman."

CHAPTER 12

Faith stared at the back of the goat-bearded kid, Benny Freeze, who was leading her mare at the tail end of the cutthroat pack, and imagined having a gun in her hand and blowing a neat round hole through the kid's ratty buffalo coat.

Her heart quickened at the imagined sound of the gun's bark and then watching her hand slide around as she blasted the others out of their saddles.

When all the men were writhing on the ground in imagined death throes, a chill breeze suddenly snapped Faith back to reality. She hunkered down in her buckskin coat, clamping her gloved hands more tightly to the saddle horn, and glanced at the two Colt Army revolvers jutting up on the kid's hips. His waist-length coat had been shoved back over the revolvers' grips, to allow for easy access. The grips of the left-side gun had been wrapped with faded rawhide, and into the leather of both holsters, just in front of the gun hammers, he'd carved his initials — BF.

Faith stared hard at the guns, as if willing them into her hands. If she could only get her hands on one . . .

Could she kill them all? Probably not. She probably couldn't kill even two before the others drilled her. Still, it was a game she'd been playing since they'd hit the trail at dawn that morning, to take her mind off what had happened back at the ranch and to quell her own worries about what awaited her at the end of the trail in Colorado.

Not what, but who . . .

Bill Thornton.

The breeze swirled the dust the horses were kicking up. Slitting her eyes, she cast a look behind her, which was another thing she'd been doing all morning — looking and wishing, half expecting Yakima to be thundering after her atop his black mustang.

Why shouldn't she expect that? Hadn't he ridden after her in Colorado, the first time Thornton had sicced a bounty hunter on her, and led her to safety?

In Mexico, Yakima had done the same when all the odds — rurales, Apaches, revolutionaries, banditos, and even a broiling underground river — were stacked against her. He'd gotten her and her brother through, even given them a home.

In her mind's eye, she saw Yakima dragged from his stirrup, the bullet wound in his head glistening, and Wolf dragging him off over the sage- and piñon-stippled hogbacks, and out of sight.

Away from her, most likely, forever.

Turning forward, she glanced once more at the guns jutting from the kid's holsters but was jolted from her violent fantasy when the mare crested a rise between two towering stone monoliths, and started down the other side, jerked into a trot by the kid. A couple of buildings appeared in the hollow below — a bowl sheathed in bald, craggy ridges.

On the bowl's left side lay a long, L-shaped log cabin with stone steps rising to a broad front porch. From a large fieldstone chimney on the building's far side, smoke tinged with the aromatic tang of mesquite fluttered like a gray flag in the cool, midday breeze.

On the bowl's right side lay a couple of corrals, sun-blistered outbuildings, and dilapidated wagons, the corrals falling down and growing up with wiry brown brush, Spanish bayonet, and prickly pear. Crows like a string of black beads perched atop a log hut with a rusted tin roof. A scruffy tabby cat sat on the splintered sideboard of one of the wagons, staring intently into the brush, its tail curling and uncurling with predatory menace.

As Faith's mare followed the other mounts toward the cabin, she saw five saddled horses standing before the two hitch rails, swishing their tails and rippling their withers. A freight wagon stood on the other side of the cabin, near a stock tank, the team of four mules eating from the feed sacks draped over their ears.

One of the saddle horses lifted a whinny and Kooch Manley's blue roan replied in kind. Above the porch a long plank sign, splattered white with bird droppings, read SAND CREEK CAFÉ AND STAGE STATION.

Smaller letters to one side announced ANGUS HAGEN, PROP., only the word ANGUS was crossed out and above it was scribbled, in different colored letters, WIDOW.

"What do you suppose happened to *Mr.* Hagen?" asked Benny Freeze as he pulled up to the left hitch rail and then drew Faith's mare up beside him.

"Killed by Apaches, most likely," opined Kooch Manley as he swung down from his saddle with a weary groan.

"Or the senora herself," Chulo Garza

150

laughed, shucking his rifle from the saddle boot.

"Hope the widow's food's as good as it was when we swung through a few days ago," Frank Miller said, rolling his thick, muscular shoulders and arms as he wound his reins around the hitch rail. "Damn, but that pot roast was good!"

As the others stretched, tied their mounts, and loosened saddle cinches, Faith glanced around at the outbuildings and then again at the five other horses and the freight wagons. Her heartbeat quickened hopefully — the horses and wagons meant there were other men here, men who might help her — until she looked down to her left.

Lowry Temple stood gazing up at her, a taut smile on his tattooed face. She'd noticed that the green cross seemed to change colors with his mood. Now it was blue black, and it appeared to be sunk deep in his windburned skin.

As he pulled out his bowie knife and cut the rawhide tying Faith's hands to the saddle horn — deciding that her hands were enough, he no longer tied her ankles to her stirrups — he said, "We're gonna go in and have us a nice sit-down meal."

The rawhide gave between her wrists, but he continued drilling his hard eyes into hers.

"You'll be my wife. A well-behaved woman. You'll sit beside me, keep your head down, and you won't speak to anyone."

Faith told him to do something physically impossible to himself. Then she swung down from the saddle and swatted dust from her denim-clad legs with her hat. Ignoring Temple hooking his arm out for her, she ducked under the hitch rail and strode along the front of the porch toward the steps.

Benny Freeze and Kooch Manley were climbing the stone steps. Frank Miller and Chulo Garza stood at the bottom, Garza casting his cautious gaze around the yard while biting the end off a cheap cigar. Miller was turned toward Faith and Lowry coming up behind her.

"If you get to play her man today, Temple," he chuckled, keeping his voice low so he wouldn't be heard inside, "can I be her man tonight?"

Faith ignored his leer as she brushed past him and mounted the porch steps. Behind her, Temple said, "You wouldn't want her today, Frank. She's in one o' them high-blooded moods given to her sex."

"I could soften her up."

"No," muttered Garza, bringing up the rear as the other three followed Faith onto the porch. "It takes a *real* man to take the edge off a catamount like that, uh? A *Mejican* bull is required, amigos. Look how she swings those hips. *Ay caramba!*"

As Faith stepped through the door, she heard the rustle and a soft thud of someone getting slapped with a hat behind her. Garza and Miller chuckled again and then fell silent as they, too, entered the dark, smoky room around which a dozen or so square, oilcloth-covered tables were arranged.

Faith stopped a few feet inside the door, blinking against the smoke and waiting for her eyes to adjust. Deep, gravelly voices rose on her left and right, filling the cavelike, low-ceilinged room. As her vision cleared, she saw four beefy gents sitting at a large table against the left wall, and three more men — range riders, judging by their chaps, dusters, and fur jackets — to her right.

At the back of the room stretched a counter with a couple of wooden stools, and behind the counter a stocky woman in a shapeless frock, her silver hair in a bun, was frying steaks and onions while what looked like beans dribbled out from beneath the lid of a large cast-iron pot. A plump, young Chinese man in a pajama-like silk jacket and oversized denim trousers carried three plates out from behind the counter, the steaks still sizzling as he set them before the three men to the right.

Freeze and Manley were dragging out chairs at a table against the left wall, about midway down the room, tossing their hats onto the chairs beside them. As the other three cutthroats muttered behind Faith, Temple came up beside her, wrapped his hand around her arm, giving a painful squeeze, and nodded at a table just beyond Freeze and Manley.

"That one'll do — won't it, honey?"

Garza and Miller brushed past them, heading for the table. Faith stepped forward, wincing as Temple gave her arm another pinch. As she walked to the right of the outlaw leader, she noticed in the corner of her eyes the other men in the room giving her curious, appraising glances.

As she passed the three men to her right — two with their backs to the wall, one with his back to her — she saw that the man with his back to her wore a silver-plated pistol in a black holster thonged low on his striped trouser leg, just above a black, mule-eared boot hooked beneath his chair. She slid her gaze up from the man's leg and saw, pinned to the open deer-hide coat of the man on the other side of the table, a copper star in which ARIZONA RANGER had been stamped.

Faith's heart thumped. Just before she turned away, led by Temple's firm hand, she saw the man gazing at her over the coffee mug he held in both his big brown hands, his trimmed gray mustache moving up and down as he chewed, his gray-blue eyes appraising her with keen male interest.

Turning her head forward, she caught a glimpse of another badge pinned to the vest of the man sitting beside the gray-mustached man, and her heart hammered harder.

Temple pulled a chair out for her. When she'd sat down and was jerking her chair toward the table, she nervously raked her eyes across the cutthroats' faces.

They didn't appear to have seen the badges. They joked and grunted as they took their seats, adjusting their guns and knife sheaths and poking their hats back off their foreheads or digging into shirt pockets for makings sacks. Frank Miller tilted back his chair, nudging the chair of Benny Freeze behind him, and Freeze gave Miller an elbow between his shoulder blades. Miller swatted him back, and Temple, sitting to Faith's right — she sat facing the front of the roadhouse — admonished them to act their ages and not their shoe sizes.

Faith cut her eyes to the three Rangers,

assuming the third man, whose chest she couldn't see from this angle, was also a lawman. They were big, capable-looking men. Getting on a little in years, maybe, but they all wore tied-down holsters from which big pistols jutted. Three rifles — two Henry repeaters and a Winchester — leaned against the wall behind their table.

A cream Stetson adorned with a red feather was hooked over the barrel of one of the Winchesters. The rifles were stock-worn and well oiled. Rifles that had, no doubt, taken down their share of border toughs like Temple and the others.

"Ho-ho. You like?"

Faith had been so intent on her desire to seek the Rangers' help, staring at the lawmen out the corner of her eye, that she hadn't noticed the young, round-faced Chinaman move up beside Temple. He held a small notebook and a pencil as he stared subserviently down at the oilcloth, waiting.

"Speaky English, China boy?" asked Manley, scowling belligerently up at the waiter from the other table.

"No much, see?" he chirped, sweat glistening on his almond features. He glanced around quickly, smiling, showing a chipped front tooth. "Steak, beans?"

"I want roast beef," ordered Manley.

"Give me potatoes and carrots with it. Slice of pie for dessert. You got peach? You had peach a couple weeks ago."

"Ho." The young man nodded, scribbling on the pad in his hand.

Faith was so intently staring at the young man's pencil — she needed to get a message to the lawmen, but she had nothing to write on or with — that she didn't realize all the others had ordered and that the young Chinaman was staring down at the table near Faith, waiting politely, before Temple said, "My wife will have steak and potatoes. Chop-chop, eh, boy? We got some ridin' ahead."

"Ho-ho," the young man said, squinting at the pad and scribbling. "Steak . . . potato. Ho-ho. Good!"

Then he shuffled quickly off toward the old woman in the kitchen, and Miller said, "Ho-Ho," and the others chuckled.

The young man returned with stone mugs of coffee, and set them in front of the outlaws and Faith. When he'd scampered off once more, in answer to the old woman's ordering bark for clean plates, Garza spiced his coffee from a small, hide-covered flask. Before he could slip the flask back into his coat, Miller grabbed it out of his hand. The thick-necked blond grinned as he tipped

157

the liquor into his own coffee, then handed the flask across the table to Temple, his cobalt blue eyes flashing crazily.

"Chrissakes, Chulo," the lead bounty hunter said, shaking his head with mock disgust. "Ain't I taught you no manners at all?"

Garza cursed, frowning at the flask, which Temple held out to Faith, cocking a brow. "Shot?"

Holding her mug in both hands in front of her chin, Faith blew on the hot, coal black belly wash. "No, thanks. I'll wait till I'm shut of you boys. Then I'll celebrate."

Temple and Miller chuckled, and Garza cursed, narrowing those dark, deep-set eyes at her as he took the flask back from Temple and tucked it back into his coat.

Faith sneered at the Mexican and, sipping her coffee, glanced casually around the dim room. Plumes of tobacco smoke rose from the freighters' table and from that of the Arizona Rangers. A loud conversational din filled the room, echoing off the log walls.

Faith glanced around casually, her mind racing, squeezing her stone coffee mug between her sweat-slick hands.

Behind her, the fire in the cookstove snapped and wheezed, and the old woman hummed softly to herself while the young

Chinaman busily scrubbed plates in a tin dishpan. The beans bubbled and a coffeepot chugged. Outside, one of the mules brayed and another answered.

"Ah, shit," groaned one of the freighters, raking his chair back from his table. "Sounds like Bennie and Jim are gettin' into it again!"

He rose heavily from his chair — a heavy, bald gent with broad hips and shoulders — and, shrugging into his knee-length buffalo coat and donning his felt sombrero, sauntered through the door and outside.

"What do you suppose he's gonna do to her?" Garza said, grinning at Faith from across the table. He was turned sideways in his chair, a boot hiked on a knee, twin plumes of blue cigar smoke jetting from both pitted nostrils.

"Who?" Miller asked, his voice just audible above the room's low, conversational roar.

"Thornton — who do you think?" Garza grunted. "Santa Claus?"

"I think he's gonna have some fun with her," Miller rasped, dipping his chin to his chest and regarding Faith from beneath his thin white brows. He raked his weird blue eyes across her amply filled blouse showing through the unbuttoned flaps of her mackinaw. "A whole lot of fun . . . before" — he ran a finger across his neck, a quick slashing motion just above his knotted green neckerchief — "he cuts her throat from ear to ear!"

Garza laughed. Lounging back in his chair and chewing as much as smoking a cheap cigar, Temple scowled and looked around to make sure no one had seen or heard.

Faith suppressed a shudder as she set her coffee mug down — chilled as much by the prospect of meeting Thornton again as by Temple realizing he was sitting ten feet away from Arizona Rangers.

She took her slightly shaking hands away from the coffee mug. "While you boys think about it," she said, "I think I'll use the privy."

"Now look what you did, Miller!" Garza slapped the blond hardcase's shoulder with the back of his hand. "You got her so frightened she has dampened her drawers!"

As Faith slid her chair back and rose, Temple casually turned to her, grabbing her wrist and tipping his head back to smile up at her through the smoke wafting from his cigar. "Now, honey, do you really think I'd let you tramp around alone back there? This is Apache and cutthroat country. No tellin' what might happen."

He winked at her mockingly, then glanced at Miller. Keeping his voice low and mild, he said, "Go with her. But leave her alone or I'll cut your nuts off."

"Why do I have to go?" Miller complained, canting his head toward Garza. "Why not him?"

" 'Cause I'm sendin' you," Temple growled.

When Miller had gained his feet, cursing under his breath and taking a long sip of his whiskey-laced coffee, Temple released Faith's hand. She turned and headed toward the door to the left of the kitchen counter and the stove, hearing Miller's thudding heels and chinking spurs behind her.

As she neared the back counter, she spied the young Chinaman's notepad and pencil, which she had seen a minute ago, when she'd raked her gaze casually behind her. The pad and pencil lay at the left end of the counter, about four feet to the right of Faith's path to the back door.

Her pulse sang in her ears as she eyed the stubby brown pencil, its lead dulled to a round nub. That's all she needed. She could find something to write on in the privy. But how could she grab the pencil with Miller right behind her?

161

CHAPTER 13

When Faith was about three feet from the counter, she saw the chair angled out from the table just ahead and to the right of her. She angled toward it while turning her head as if to inspect a small heliograph on the wall to her left.

She caught a leg of the chair with the toe of her right boot, and stumbled forward, pushing slightly off her left foot and throwing herself up against the counter. She gave a mock-startled groan and closed her hand over the pencil.

"Jesus," she grunted.

"Christ, girl," Miller chuckled behind her. "I guess beauty and grace don't necessarily go together."

She pushed off the counter, palming the pencil and furtively poking it into her hip pocket, scowling up at Miller while blowing a wisp of hair from her eye.

"Grace and beauty — I reckon that's your

department, Miller."

She looked behind the stocky blond to see the three Rangers glancing at her out the corner of their eyes and chuckling bemusedly. Apparently, her own gang hadn't seen the maneuver, because Temple and Garza were conversing with Manley and Benny Freeze at the table behind them.

The burly freighter had just entered the roadhouse again, and his bulky hobnailed boots pounded the floorboards, and his deep voice boomed as he announced, "I think Bennie was tryin' to get into Jim's feed sack again — the pigheaded devil! Sneakier'n a reservation 'Pache!"

Faith gave Miller a caustic snort and continued past the end of the counter.

Feeling the slim, solid pencil nestled inside her pocket, she pushed through the back door and into the sunny, dusty lot behind the roadhouse. She strode past a pile of split wood, frightening a coyote that had been scavenging a trash pile farther out in the shrubs, and headed for the single-hole privy standing beneath a leafless gray cottonwood.

"Need any help?" Miller asked, moseying along behind her, kicking a rusty can.

"Don't get your hopes up."

Swallowing the dry knot in her throat,

Faith opened the squeaky privy door. Inside, the smell of human waste was almost suffocating. She closed the door and punched the locking nail home, then looked around quickly. A pile of time-yellowed dime novels lay on the warped boards to the left of the hole.

Faith reached for one of the paper-covered books, which the large black letters on the front announced as THE ADVENTURES OF PISTOL PETE AND ARIZONA KATE. Below the title was a sketch of a man and a woman leaning out from their horses to kiss each other on the lips.

There was a sharp *crack,* almost as loud as a pistol shot, and Faith jerked with a gasp. For a second she thought that Miller had fired a shot at the privy. But then, hearing him chuckle, she realized he'd thrown a rock at the door.

"Sorry," the thick-necked blond said in a mocking, nasal twang. "Hope I didn't scare ya."

"Your pa must have spared the rod, Miller," Faith said, swallowing again and taking a deep breath to quell her hammering heart.

"That he shore did," Miller said. "I reckon he was too busy with girls like you to much care what his boy was doin'. Yessir, I had the run of the town!"

Another rock barked against the privy door. Faith's hand jerked away from the book once more, and she bit back a curse as she glared through the cracks between the privy's vertical boards at the stocky figure milling about the wood pile, kicking rocks, and chuckling.

"Quite the idyllic childhood," Faith said, leaning forward once more to pluck the book from the top of the stack.

"You could say that," Miller allowed.

She quickly sat back over the hole, laid the book in her lap, and threw back the cover to the title page. Beneath the title, the ink bleeding from copper-colored water stains, there were a good three inches of white space. As Miller continued yammering out in the yard, his voice rising and falling as he turned this way and that, bored and owly as a schoolyard bully, Faith pulled the pencil out of her pocket.

Trying in vain to keep her hand from shaking, she touched the nub to her tongue, then pressed the lead to the rough pulp paper, scribbling quickly. She kept the note short and simple, merely telling the Rangers who she was and that she'd been abducted and she'd appreciate their help.

She signed her name at the bottom, having barely made room for it. She'd no sooner finished before she quickly jerked her head up with a soft gasp.

Outside rose the soft ring of a boot spur, and then Miller said something too low for her to hear. Another man said something in a raspy, slightly high-pitched voice.

Faith leaned forward from the throne and turned her head this way and that, peering through the cracks between the boards. Miller leaned against the wood pile, muscular arms crossed on his chest, talking to someone — a man several inches taller than he — standing to one side, thumbs hooked in his back pockets.

"The girl's in there now," Miller said. "Should be done in a minute, but I ain't heard from her. She mighta fallen in."

He and the other man chuckled. Faith squinted through a crack just right of the door. As the taller man turned slightly toward the privy, tobacco smoke puffing around his gray-mustached face, the brassy sunlight flashed off something shiny on his chest.

A badge.

Faith cursed softly. It was one of the Rangers. Now Miller and the others would know about the lawmen.

Faith swallowed quickly and looked around, wondering what to do. Then she stared calmly through the crack once more. Miller and the Ranger conversed in a desultory way, the Ranger yawning and lifting his hat to run a hand through his thick silver hair.

What was she worried about? The man was about to use the privy. That took care of the problem of how to get him the note!

Faith looked around for a place to put the note so the Ranger wouldn't miss it. She could set it to either side of the hole, but there was a chance the breeze sifting through the tracks might blow it onto the floor and he'd mistake it for trash.

She looked at the door's latching nail. Her chest fluttered as though butterflies had just hatched in her belly. Leaning forward, she gently lifted the nail from the eye and impaled the note over the nail's sharp end.

When she was sure the note was going to stay on the nail and not slither off to the floor, she stood straight, smoothed her hair back from her cheek, sucked a deep, calming breath, and pushed out through the door.

"There she is!" Miller said, leaning against the wood pile, arms crossed on his chest. He glanced at the tall, gray-haired Ranger standing nearby. "Lookee here, got us an Arizona Ranger. Miss Faith, meet Ranger

Jake Winter."

Faith's heart fluttered as she cut her eyes between the grinning Miller and the Ranger, whose leathery face flushed slightly as he nodded cordially, then, as an afterthought, reached up to remove his hat. "Ma'am."

Faith nodded back as she passed between the two men. "How do you do?"

"Well, better now that you finally freed up the outhouse!" Miller chuckled. Then he tipped his hat to the Ranger, who gave an official smile as he set his hat on his head and began tramping toward the outhouse, looking goosey on his long, slightly stiff legs clad in brown-checked wool.

Reaching for the back door handle, Faith glanced quickly over her shoulder, her heart now skipping beats as the Ranger reached for the handle of the outhouse door. Just as the man began drawing the door open, Faith stepped into the roadhouse and strode straight on past a couple of hanging brooms and the counter to the table where the others were hunkered over steaming plates and coffee mugs.

" 'Bout time," Temple said, pulling Faith's chair out with one hand. "Your food's gettin' cold."

"Can't turn a deaf ear to nature's call."

Faith sat down and, scooting her chair

forward, looked down at her plate. The steak was swimming in its own grease, a dollop of butter melting on top. At any other time after a long, hard ride, the succulent beef, cooked the way she liked it — rare — would have made her mouth water and her stomach growl hungrily.

Now, with her stomach in knots, the sight and smell of the food nearly made her wretch.

In spite of herself, she picked up her fork and knife and began cutting into the meat. At the same time, Miller leaned toward Temple, who was hungrily shoving steak and potatoes into his mouth.

"Did you see . . . ?" the blond said so softly that Faith could barely hear. Miller canted his head toward the two Rangers sitting on the other side of the room, fifteen feet away.

"I saw the badge when one got up," Temple said, keeping his own voice low, below the din of the laughing freighters and the two Rangers themselves, who appeared in serious and somewhat heated discussion, the words "reservation" and "redskin" occasionally rising above their table.

Temple swallowed and turned to Faith, who was forcing a small bite of meat into her mouth. He wore his nerve-cleaving, insinuating smile. "You didn't know we were sharing the room with law dogs, did you?"

"Not until a minute ago," Faith said, purposefully chewing the meat and trying to look as though she were enjoying it. "Wish I had. I would have leaped onto the table and begged them to shoot you out of your damn boots."

She swallowed and dipped her fork into her buttery baked potato. Across from her, Garza was as busy shoveling food as Temple, to whom he growled, "Wouldn't worry, *jefe.* It's only three old coyotes. I'll take them out as soon as I'm done eating, if you wish."

"No trouble," Temple said. "We got a job to do, and we ain't gonna complicate it. Besides, they ain't done nothin' to us."

"Yes, well, they are lawmen just the same." Chulo grinned, showing the food stuck to his rotten, crooked teeth. "You know how I feel about lawmen, uh?"

Behind Faith, the back door opened with a slight screech. Boots thudded and scuffed, and then the door rasped shut. Though she'd been listening for the lawman's return, Faith jerked with a start.

She stared hard at her plate, trying to keep her hands moving, as she heard the loudening clomp of boots and *ching* of spurs. When the Ranger appeared to Temple's left, angling toward the table where the other two lawmen were now drinking coffee and eating cobbler, she cast a quick glance toward that side of the room. The Ranger, Winter, stood across from one of the others, and tapped the crown of the man's black hat.

"Ain't polite, you know, Grayson — wearin' your hat inside." Winter chuckled and, without so much as a glance in Faith's direction, dragged out his chair, doffed his own hat, and sat down to the table. "Didn't your ma teach ya nothin'?"

Good, Faith thought, as the lawmen casually conversed, Winter digging into the pie that had been waiting for him. Play it cool. She'd been worried they might make a play on the cutthroats as soon as they found out her situation, and get themselves killed.

But they were too savvy for that. They were Rangers, after all. Not local tin stars with reputations to build. They'd talk it over, bide their time, and wait for the right moment to make their move.

"Ain't hungry?" Temple said later, when the young Chinaman had set dessert before each of them and refilled their coffee mugs.

Faith glanced down. She'd eaten only half her steak and potato and only a few bites of her green beans. She'd turned down dessert and was now only sipping her coffee.

"It isn't like I have a barn to clean today," she muttered, raising her mug to her lips.

"Got a long pull ahead." Miller shoved a forkful of cream-drenched pie into his mouth, and chewed with his mouth open. "Best eat up. Build your strength for Thornton."

She opened her mouth to respond, but stopped when, on the other side of the room, the Rangers all raked their chairs back and, sighing and stifling belches, plunked coins onto the table. They buttoned their coats, donned their hats, hefted their rifles, and started toward the door.

The man called Grayson cast a glance at the back of the room. "Thanks, Edna. Be back through next week, prob'ly."

"You be good, Dave!" the old woman called without turning from scrubbing the range top.

"He couldn't be good if there was money in it," Winter called, laughing and resting his rifle on his shoulder as he opened the door.

The freighters had already left, and when the lawmen had thumped on out of the roadhouse and off the porch, joking and laughing as they tightened their saddle cinches outside, a cavelike silence descended. It was broken only by the ticks of the cutthroats' forks, their snorts, and the raucous scrape of Garza sliding back his chair and scratching a lucifer to light on his large-roweled Chihuahua spur.

Benny Freeze groaned and stretched. "Jeepers, now I could use a nap!"

Faith stared over her coffee mug, between Miller and Garza, and out the bright window at the far end of the room's smoky purple shadows. The Rangers, still conversing easily, had mounted their horses. The one named Grayson paused while the others pulled their horses away from the hitch rail to light his cigar. Then he reined his bay around and followed the others out of the yard, heading in the direction from which Faith and the others had come.

Faith stared at the dust wafting in the yard before the window, incredulity mixing with the tension in her gut. She'd thought the men were merely acting casual, so as not to telegraph their intent to the cutthroats. But now she was beginning to doubt that Winter had found her note in the privy.

The Rangers hadn't seemed to be acting. They hadn't hesitated once. Not one had glanced suspiciously toward Faith or her kidnappers. And when they'd ridden from the yard, they'd done so with purposeful ease, eyes intent on the trail before them.

Suddenly, she felt Temple's gray eyes on her, and she glanced at the outlaw leader. "Damn," he said, lifting his mouth corners shrewdly. "They're gone. And you're still here . . . on your way to see an old friend."

Faith bit the inside of her lip, feeling the burn of frustration and anger down deep in her loins. Then she turned away and, maintaining a casual air, threw back the last of her coffee.

"Time to pull foot, fellas," Temple said, rising and dropping his spent cheroot in his coffee mug, where it fizzled softly. He and the others dropped coins on the table with a metallic clatter.

Rising from her own chair, Faith glanced once more at the Rangers' table, which the young Chinaman was busily clearing. Her note must have slipped off the privy door's locking nail when either she or the Ranger had opened the door, and the breeze had no doubt blown it away. If he'd seen the scrap, he'd probably dismissed it as trash.

Frustration bit her, and she silently cursed herself for a fool. Three lawmen had been no more than fifteen feet away from her, and her own carelessness had foiled her attempt at summoning their help.

"Come on, *dearest*," Temple ordered,

grabbing her arm and shoving her toward the door. "Quit lollygaggin' and break a leg."

CHAPTER 14

Temple tightened Faith's mare's saddle cinch, and then he tied Faith's wrists to her saddle horn. He and the others mounted, and as the sun began angling westward from its zenith and a cool breeze swept dust from the yard, the group headed north from the roadhouse, the faint clatter of pots and pans echoing behind them.

Riding through high mountain country, pines shading their trail as they climbed toward a steep rimrock formation, eagles screeching over a stream winking in the valley they'd just left, Faith found her thoughts returning to Yakima and her brother, Kelly.

Both dead now, she was sure. If Yakima wasn't dead, he would have tracked her by now. She was sure of it. It was just as well she hadn't been able to summon the Rangers' help. Why put others in danger? She no longer cared what happened to her.

Besides her, Kelly had been the last living

member of her immediate family. Her older brother, George, had been killed in a ranching accident somewhere in Wyoming, and her father, who had been living alone in the Chugwater Buttes north of Cheyenne, had drunk himself to death. Her mother had died of a fever a year before Faith had left home at age fifteen — driven out by her father's bereaved, drunken rage.

Now the only man she'd ever loved had been taken from her, too. Her chest heaved suddenly with a raw wave of sorrow, and, as she'd trained herself over her long run of hard years, she quickly turned it to anger. She set her jaws and imagined the face of the man responsible.

Bill Thornton.

A mild voice interrupted her thoughts — a voice so soft and mild that at first she thought she'd imagined it or that it had been a trick of the wind. Temple must have wondered, too, because, ahead of Faith's mare, he turned his head slowly from side to side, a curious frown ridging his brow.

"Temple," Miller said, riding just off Faith's mare's right hip.

The outlaw leader pulled back on his steeldust's reins and started turning toward Miller when something in the rocks right of the trail caught his eye, and his right hand dropped to one of his revolvers.

The voice came again, louder this time. "Uh-uh. Nope. That's the wrong thing to do, mister."

Faith whipped her head around quickly, at first thinking they'd been stopped by bandits. But then the sun glinted dully off a badge, and her pulse quickened.

The Ranger she'd met behind the road-house, Winter, was aiming a rifle out from behind a scarp amongst the pines behind her and right of the trail, upslope a few yards. Another Ranger — the one called Grayson — stood beside a tree ahead and just to the left of the trail, slightly down-slope. He aimed a Winchester straight out from his shoulder, while the third man, who had gray hair like Winter's and an even more sun-darkened face, aimed his own rifle from the same scarp as did Winter, but ahead and to the right of the trail. A long weed stem protruded from between his teeth.

"What is this?" Temple grunted.

"Arizona Rangers. You fellas raise your hands, and do it fast. Any detours on the way to clawing air is gonna get you drilled deader'n hell."

"Must be some mistake," Manley laughed, swinging his head around. "We ain't done nothin' wrong."

"Get your hands raised," said Ranger Grayson, his rifle stock and low-canted black hat brim hiding his face. "Anyone tries to bolt, you're dead."

The cutthroats looked around at each other, and then, at the same time, Garza and Temple swung their heads toward Faith, their expressions both wry and accusing.

Dropping their reins, they and the others raised their hands above their shoulders. Temple dropped Faith's lead line and the mare convulsed slightly, startled.

Miller chuckled dryly. "What the hell is this bullshit?"

Winter barked at Garza. "You! Mex! Real slow — I mean slow as chilled honey — take that knife of yours, ride over, and cut the lady free of her saddle. Any quick movements, and I'll drill one through your brisket."

"He's a good shot," Grayson said. "And I'm even better."

Garza glanced from Grayson to Winter and back again, letting his eyes rake across the man hunkered between them. The Mexican's hair blew out from his face like two shaggy blackbird wings, and his nostrils flared. He spat savagely and reached for the knife handle jutting high on his right hip, above his coat.

"Slowww," the third Ranger warned, momentarily releasing his grip on his Henry's forestock to flick a fly away with his fingers.

Garza wrapped his fingers around the big, bone-handled bowie and, scowling at the Ranger who'd just spoken, slowly lifted the blade free of its sheath. He gigged his horse over to Faith's mare and leaned toward her.

"I'm drawing a bead between your shoulders, mister," Winter warned. "Just so's ya know. . . ."

Garza slowly extended the knife toward Faith's saddle. The Mexican stared hard into her eyes, his own eyes black with mute fury, his bourbon-colored, broad-nosed features like granite. He set the curved blade tip between Faith's wrists and against the rawhide, then flicked the blade back toward himself.

Faith jerked with a start, certain he would bury the blade in her belly. The rawhide fell away. Holding her gaze with his, Garza slowly pulled the knife back, straightening his back.

"It's a hot potato," Winter said, all three Rangers still bearing down with their rifles. "Throw it down."

Garza snorted. "Hot-hot!" he said suddenly, causing the Rangers to jerk their rifle barrels with frightened starts. Chuckling, the Mex bounty hunter tossed the knife into the grass beside the trail.

"Miss, you ride on over here," Winter ordered, lifting his head a little but continuing to squint down his Winchester's barrel.

Faith reached down and grabbed her reins, then, glancing cautiously at the cutthroats, none of whom was looking at her now, turned the mare around. She gigged the mount over toward Winter. When she was back behind the man and the rock escarpment, she lowered herself from the saddle and, crouching, still wary of a lead swap, moved up beside him and dropped to a knee.

"You got my note."

Winter nodded. "Didn't want to let on. We had them pegged for trouble as soon as they walked in, but none of us remembered seein' paper on 'em."

Faith lifted her gaze to where the cutthroats were now, per Ranger Grayson's orders, slowly tossing down a virtual armory of pistols, knives, and rifles. When they'd finished, they began, one by one, dismounting.

"Be careful," Faith whispered to Winter, pressing her clenched hands to her chest, feeling her heart's frenetic rhythm through her breastbone.

Winter glanced at Faith, his thick gray mustache rising slightly as he offered a reassuring smile. "You're all right now, miss. Sit tight till I come back for you."

Faith whispered again, beseeching the man to be careful. He stepped out from behind the scarp, lowering his rifle as he moved a few steps into the clearing where the only outlaw left mounted was Frank Miller, who'd begun singing "Oh, Susannah."

"Keep your mouth shut," Winter told him, holding his Winchester straight out from his hip.

"I beg your pardon, Ranger," Miller said. "But I always sing when I'm nervous."

Faith watched from one knee, peering around the scarp, as Grayson ordered Miller out of the saddle. Then all five cutthroats were facedown in the middle of the trail, their horses milling slightly down the slope behind them, a couple of the mounts watching their masters curiously while others grazed and swished their tails, oblivious.

Grayson and the third Ranger, whom one of the others had called Hodges, had kicked the bounty hunters' weapons out of reach.

Miller continued singing, one cheek

pressed to the ground, as Winter and Hodges kept the cutthroats covered as Grayson approached the group, two pairs of handcuffs dangling from his left hand.

"Careful," Winter warned as Grayson took his rifle under one arm and crouched over Lowry Temple.

The lead bounty hunter had said nothing since Faith had ridden over to Winter, but had stiffly, automatically followed the Rangers' orders, a chilling look of serenity etched on his face.

She held her breath as Grayson dropped to a knee beside Temple. What happened next happened so quickly that Faith's mind was about two seconds behind it, her stunned brain trying to make sense of the images her eyes were sending it.

A half second after Garza had lifted his head suddenly, gritting his teeth, and shouting, "Manley, quit elbowing me, you fat bastard!" Temple's own head shot up. His right hand flicked up and out toward Grayson, who had jerked his head toward Manley.

Faith saw the sun flash off something shiny protruding from the underside of the outlaw leader's wrist. Temple flicked his closed fist in front of Grayson's throat, as though he were brushing away a fly.

Grayson's head jerked back and, haltingly, he straightened and stumbled backward, his rifle falling from beneath his arm as he grabbed his throat.

At the same time, in a blur of movement, Miller rolled sideways, turning completely over, his right hand flicking toward his chest and then up and out toward Winter, squinting over his clenched fist.

Winter tensed, his head jerking right to left and back again, and Faith saw his lower jaw drop as though he were about to say something. But no words left his mouth before the small gun in Miller's fist cracked, like the sound of a jawbreaker broken in a kid's mouth, and smoke and flames stabbed.

"No!" Faith screamed as Winter jerked back and sideways with a startled grunt. He triggered his rifle, and Manley jerked his head down, cursing.

Ranger Hodges shouted something unintelligible and fired his own rifle, blowing up dirt and gravel in front of Miller, and then, hair flying wildly, Garza bolted up and forward and was pushing Grayson into Hodges as the third Ranger was trying to lever another round into his Henry's breech.

Howling like a lobo, Garza pulled Grayson's revolver from his holster, snaked it around Grayson's sagging body, which blood from his neck was now lathering thickly, and fired two quick shots into Hodges's belly.

Holding the Ranger's smoking revolver in his hand, Garza howled demonically as both men fell in groaning heaps before him.

Faith raked her shocked gaze from them to Winter as the leather-faced Ranger stumbled over a rock and fell on his back ten feet in front of her. Blood pumped from the ragged hole in his upper left chest, coating his badge. His flat belly rose and fell heavily, and his gray-blue eyes sparked in the sunlight as he tipped his head back and wheezed, "Run!"

Faith realized she hadn't drawn a breath in the five seconds that had elapsed since Garza's first shout, and now, wheeling from the rocks, she sucked a shallow one and bolted into the pines. Her heart pumped and her arms scissored and she could hear her own small, anxious grunts and the grass and pine needles crunching beneath her boots as she ran blindly, aimlessly, trying to put as much distance between her and the cutthroats as she could.

Boots tapped faintly behind her.

She gasped, continued running along the base of a rimrock angling back away from the trail and into scrub brush and dwarf pines. The boot taps became thuds, growing louder until they were joined with the heavy rasps of labored breaths.

Faith was about to look behind her when her pursuer, closing on her fast, reached out to give her a violent shove. She stumbled and fell, the ground coming up hard against her hip and shoulder, and rolled.

Someone pulled her up brusquely by her hair, making her scalp burn. In her swimming vision, she saw Lowry Temple staring down at her, that stony, savage look again in his eyes, the small tattooed cross obscured by bulging skin in his forehead.

His arm swung back and forward, and he slapped her hard with an open palm. He slapped her again with the back of the same hand, and she flew backward, tripping over a rock, her head hammering and her vision dimming.

Slipping in and out of consciousness, her scalp and her cheeks burning, Faith was vaguely aware of being carried over someone's shoulder. Then the movement stopped for a half second, and, slitting her eyes, she saw rocks and gravel and sage tufts fly up toward her to smack her head and shoulders. The fall — or the throw, rather, for she realized that Temple had tossed her like so much trash into the trail around which the three Rangers lay unmoving — somewhat braced her.

She lifted her head.

Temple, Benny Freeze, and Chulo Garza stood around Frank Miller, who lay writhing on the ground in their elongated shadows, grunting and showing his teeth while clutching both hands to his belly. Nearby, Kooch Manley squatted at the base of the scarp, pouring water from his canteen into the bloody gash at the top of his nearly bald skull.

There was a soft hissing to the right. Ranger Winter had grabbed his Winchester and was trying to lift it off the ground while trying to work the cocking lever, his pain-racked, sweat-soaked face a mask of misery and rage.

Kooch Manley dropped his canteen, palmed his revolver, and fired.

The bullet took Winter through the middle of his forehead and threw him back hard. One upraised knee jerked before slowly dropping and lying still.

Grumbling, Manley crouched to pluck his canteen out of the grass. He cursed and glanced at the others still hovering around the groaning Miller.

"Now look!" The middle-aged cutthroat held up his canteen. "On top of everything else, I spilled my water!"

Temple shoved Benny Freeze aside so he could get a better look at Miller. "How bad is it, Frank?"

"It's bad," Freeze answered for him. "Jackie Burnside took one like that when we was skinnin' out of a bank in Tascosa, and he didn't live more'n a couple hours. One hell of a painful way to go, too."

"Looks like the lawman drilled him through the belly button," Garza told Temple, shaking his head. "The bambino is right. Frank's a goner."

Miller kicked his boots in the dirt and lifted his head to peer over at Faith reclining on her elbows in the middle of the trail, her hair in her eyes. "Bitch! It's all your damn fault. Chulo, kill that whore for me. Ease my passin', and lop her damn head off!"

Garza swung toward Faith but stopped when Temple grabbed his arm. "I didn't ride all this way for nothin'. Besides, you can't blame her for tryin' to get away. We should have been ready for this."

"Only a pack of damn tinhorns would ride into that ambush." Holding a neckerchief to his head, Manley swung his canteen over his shoulder and headed toward his horse. "Tinhorns! I say we're lucky it's only Miller

188

that bought it."

While Manley strode off into the loosely clumped horses down the slope behind Faith, Temple dropped to a knee before Miller. He gave the wounded bounty hunter a meaningful look. "You ain't gonna make it, Frank."

Miller lowered his pain-pinched eyes to his bloody middle. "Leave me my horse . . . my canteen. I'll wait it out. If I think I can make it, I'll try to ride back to the roadhouse."

Temple nodded, stood, and walked over to his horse. The others followed him, glancing back at Miller, who lay slumped against a boulder beside the trail.

When Temple had led his horse and Faith's into the trail, he brusquely hauled Faith into her saddle and tied her hands to her horn. He mounted up, rode over, and dropped Miller's canteen between the stocky blond's spread legs.

"There ya are, Frank. Benny tied your horse. See ya around maybe, huh?"

Miller just cursed and plucked out the canteen's cork with his teeth.

Temple swung his horse around and jerked Faith's mare off in the direction they'd been heading before the ambush.

"Come on, fellas. Let's lift some dirt. We got a train to catch!"

Chapter 15

Moving quickly, now riding the two mustangs they'd stolen from the Apache remuda, Yakima and Brody Harms pushed hard up the rocky Mogollon Mountain trail and into the shade of towering pines. Yakima led Wolf on a lead line while Harms led a second Apache mustang.

The Easterner had slapped his mule home, and the mule hadn't hesitated.

Wolf nickered and shook his head, smelling something he didn't like. Yakima looked closely over the horse's twitching ears, then drew sharply back on the reins. Riding behind him, Harms followed suit, his leather squawking as he rose in his saddle to take his own gander.

Ahead, a man lay off to the right side of the trail, his head resting on his arm as though he were napping. Blood oozed from a couple of wounds in his chest and belly. On his vest, exposed by the open flaps of his fur coat, was an Arizona Rangers badge.

Harms's voice rose sharply. "Yakima!"

The half-breed jerked his gaze to his right. Two more men lay unmoving nearby, but Yakima fixed his gaze on a man with short blond hair and a stout neck reclining against a boulder at the base of a stone dike, a canteen propped between his legs. Staring at Yakima and Harms and gritting his teeth, the blond was fumbling a revolver from the holster jutting on his right hip.

Bright red blood soaked his belly, staining the dirt beneath his crotch, between his spread legs.

"Goddamnit!" he grunted, finally jerking the revolver free of its holster.

"This way!" Yakima shouted, neck-reining the vinegar-dun Indian pony off the trail's right side.

Harms cursed and followed suit, then cursed again as the blond's revolver barked, sending a slug buzzing through the air before spanging off a rock. There was another *pop* but not before Yakima, Harms, and their trailing horses were moving back behind a scarp, then up the slope toward the rimrock.

Yakima checked the Indian pony down behind a lightning-topped fir, and swung down from the saddle. Harms reined down his own two horses and shucked his Spencer from its saddle scabbard.

He scowled red-faced at Yakima. "You think . . . ?"

"It's one o' them." Yakima slid his Yellowboy from its scabbard. "I want him alive."

He racked a fresh shell, then quickly tied the Indian pony to a fir branch. Harms did the same and then both men jogged back down the slope toward the scarp.

"Move around from the right," Yakima said. "Make some noise but stay out of sight."

He bounded up the wall of the scarp, using clefts and cracks to pull himself up. The scarp was low, and he made the crest in seconds, crouching as he took his rifle in both hands and stared down the other side.

The stocky blond man was down on an elbow, jerking looks toward both ends of the scarp, his cocked pistol in his bloody right hand. A stone arced out from the right side of the cleft, landed with a soft bark, and rolled a few feet, drawing the outlaw's attention. Turning toward the rock, he held still long enough for Yakima to draw a bead on the hand holding the pistol.

The Yellowboy cracked.

The blond gent howled and dropped his revolver, grabbing his right hand with his left. Blood oozed from the bullet hole and dribbled into the dirt. The hardcase glared up at Yakima, who lowered the rifle and leaped down the scarp to stand in the clearing near one of the dead Rangers.

Shivering with pain and fury, the blond gent lay back on an elbow, squeezing his hand and cursing between clenched teeth. As he studied Yakima, recognition sparked in his eyes.

Yakima reached down, grabbed a Colt from the blond's second holster, and tossed it away. He planted the sole of his moccasin boot against the man's chest, and pushed him back against a rock. "Is my woman all right?"

The blond stared up at Yakima, tears of pain rolling down his cheeks, lips quivering. A savage smile quirked his mouth corners. "Yeah," he drawled mockingly. "She's just fine."

"Where are they taking her?"

Through the sharp fog of pain, the blond mulled his answer. He sucked a sharp breath through gritted teeth and renewed his grip on his shaking right hand, which was dribbling scarlet blood into the darker stuff sopping his belly. "Thornton."

The answer made his eyes dance briefly as he stared up at Yakima.

The name grabbed Yakima like a fishhook deep in his belly, and he nodded. "Had a feelin'."

The blond tipped his head back, eyes rolling back into his head. "He's . . . got plans for her . . . Thornton does."

Harms said, "Who's Thornton?"

"An old friend of ours — Faith's and mine."

Yakima looked down at the outlaw writhing before him, and pressed his boot more firmly against the man's chest. "Thornton still in Colorado?" There was the chance the pimp had made the trip to Arizona, was holed up waiting for Faith in Phoenix or Prescott.

The blond gent nodded and ground a boot heel into the dirt, groaning.

Yakima jogged past Harms on his way back toward the horses, yelling over his shoulder, "They're heading for the train rails north of here!"

"This, uh, Thornton . . . ," Harms said as he jogged, breathing hard, behind Yakima. "I assume he has a bone to pick?"

"I should have gone back and killed the bastard," Yakima growled.

He switched saddles quickly and leaped onto Wolf's back. As he and Harms galloped down the slope and onto the trail where the dead Rangers lay around the wounded blond, the bounty hunter screamed, "Breed!"

Yakima glanced over his shoulder. The blond man was reaching for the revolver Yakima had tossed into the trail. The gun was about two feet beyond his reach.

"Kick that gun over here, will ya? Last request of a dead man."

The man wanted to end his suffering.

Yakima nodded at the hide-wrapped bowie handle jutting from a sheath on the bounty hunter's left hip. "Use your knife, you son of a bitch!"

Then he and Wolf and the Apache bronc tore off down the trail, the dying outlaw raging like a trapped coyote behind him.

Yakima pushed Wolf hard. Harms pushed his own mustang just as hard, and they split the wind, angling down the pine-studded cordillera, across a wide canyon, then up onto a relatively flat stretch of high desert.

It wasn't long after leaving the canyon that they came upon a stage trail. The outlaws' prints marked the trail, and judging by the texture of the horse apples, they were only about an hour ahead. But if they hopped a train, they'd be out of reach in no time.

Yakima ground his heels into Wolf's flanks,

and he and Harms shot down the trail
through the cedars, sage, and occasional
cottonwood thickets, until they could see a
town ahead, bleeding purple shadows onto
the coppery plane. He didn't know the
town's name — if it had one. It had probably sprouted up with the coming of the
rails. Steeple Rock, blue and misty, its west
side touched with gold, loomed just beyond.

Yakima couldn't see much except a few
corrals and brick walls jutting above the
cedars, but when he and Harms topped a
rise he saw the rails — freshly laid on their
cinder bed and stretching from east to west
like twin streams of quicksilver over the low,
toffee-colored hills.

At the town's east end, inky black smoke
bled into the air. At the base of the smoke
hulked a bulky black Baldwin locomotive
with a diamond-shaped stack.

Yakima's shoulders tightened. The thickening smoke meant the fireman was stoking
the boiler, preparing to pull out.

Yakima released the Indian pony and
leaned low over Wolf's head. "Giddyap,
Wolf! Haul ass!"

The black stretched his stride, blowing
hard, pasting his ears back against his head.
Yakima, crouched low and forward, felt the
muscles rippling like snakes beneath the

saddle, saw the black withers slick with silver lather. Brody Harms and the Indian pony dropped gradually back on Yakima's right, as Yakima and the black stallion shot up the trail, lifting the town out of the salmon-tinged rocks and scrub before them.

Wolf dropped into a low area, and Yakima gritted his teeth when he heard the locomotive's dinosaur wail. Rising out of the hollow, he looked east. The train was crawling forward, great clouds of black smoke and glowing cinders wafting from the stack, steam rising from the heavy iron wheels.

Yakima cursed as he approached the town's first corrals and plank-board, tin-roofed shacks and cow pens. He checked Wolf down and turned as Brody Harms thundered up behind him, the Easterner's dusty bowler tipped low over his equally dusty spectacles.

"I'm gonna try to catch it!"

Yakima turned Wolf off the right side of the trail and into the scrub.

"You don't know for sure they're on it!" Harms yelled, his words dwindling into the distance behind Yakima, as Yakima and the black stallion pounded through the cedars and scrub junipers.

They angled around the few stock pens and shacks outlying the town, and the tent frames remaining in the wake of the railroad crew, and traced a northeastward arc toward the screeching, panting locomotive. The glistening iron horse was pulling a tender car, a couple of flatcars, and four passenger cars, with a bright yellow caboose bringing up the rear.

The engine continued to blow its shrill, bugling horn, black smoke broiling from the wide-mouthed stack as though from a barn fire. Yakima hardened his jaws as it increased its speed, singing in an ever-increasing tempo — *Whoosh-whoosh-chug! Whoosh-whoosh-chug! Whoosh-whoosh-chug!* as it slipped off away to the east, the caboose opening more and more space behind it and the freshly painted depot building and the pole corrals, which were so new that Yakima could still smell the pine resin.

The train slid away as though drawn by a giant, invisible string.

Yakima hunkered low over Wolf's neck, slitting his eyes as the wind blasted his hat brim against his forehead. "No," he spat between gritted teeth as the train gradually outdistanced him. "Goddamnit, no!"

CHAPTER 16

Wolf must have thought Yakima yelled "Go!" instead of "No!" because from somewhere deep in his wild heart, the stallion found another reserve of bronco strength.

Bounding out over the sage and plowing over stunt piñons as though they were paper, he widened his stride a few more inches, phlegm and spittle flying back from his nose like rain, hooves hammering like the locomotive's own steel pistons.

Chewing his lower lip, his green eyes blazing with a savage fire beneath his bent hat brim, Yakima watched the train suddenly stop stretching out away from him and, as though the locomotive had suddenly been shoved into reverse, fall back toward his left.

"That's it, Wolf. That's it, boy," Yakima ground out through gritted teeth as he and the stallion approached the train from ahead of the caboose, slanting toward the third passenger car.

Inside the second car, sitting next to the window and facing Lowry Temple and the car's rear, Faith sat still as a statue, numb by all that had happened.

A voice rose above the rumble of the heavy wheels beneath her feet and the low hum of conversation around her. "Jesus Christ, some crazy damn cowboy . . ."

Faith opened her eyes and glanced out the soot-stained window, and a frown bit into her forehead.

"Look at that," said someone behind her. "What's he tryin' to do — board without payin'?"

"That's one way to do it!" laughed another man.

Faith saw the rider behind the thin veil of wafting steam and wood smoke, racing toward the train on a blaze-faced black stallion.

"Gonna kill that horse," someone muttered on the other side of the car, as the horse and rider closed on the train to ride parallel, falling back gradually while inching ever closer to the tracks.

The smoke wafted away from the rider's low-canted head around which a white bandage was wrapped, and the black brim snapped up to reveal two jade green eyes in sharp contrast to the high, wide cheekbones and coffee-colored skin. Faith's heart rolled, and before she knew what she was doing, she'd leaped to her feet and bounded over Kooch Manley's knees to claw at the window, which had been closed against the flying soot and cinders.

She got it down quickly and poked her head out.

"Yakima!"

The wind, rife with wood smoke, tore the scream from her lips.

"Dios!" Garza barked. "What the hell?"

"It's the damn half-breed!" Temple had lunged to his feet and now, peering out the window, jerked Faith back with one arm and threw her brusquely into her seat.

He grabbed a revolver, thumbed back the hammer, and stuck his arm out the window. He angled the gun back along the train and slightly out to where Yakima and Wolf were still inching toward the thundering train car. They'd fallen far enough back that Faith could see only Wolf's bobbing, blaze-faced head.

"No!" she screamed, bounding back up from her seat, clawing at Temple's back. Garza smashed the back of his hand against her face, throwing her over her seat's outside armrest and into the aisle.

Outside the train, Yakima saw the arm

snake out the window, the silver-plated revolver glistening faintly in the day's waning light. He jerked his head down as the gun barked, sounding little louder than a hiccup amidst the rumbling of the car and the clattering of the wheels over the seams.

Yakima ducked again as once more the revolver stabbed flames toward him, puffing smoke. Wolf jerked to one side.

Yakima glanced at the caboose drawing up on his left. A brass rail ran along the top. As the cutthroat's gun belched once more, the slug piercing the crown of Yakima's hat, the half-breed crawled up from his stirrup to set both his boots on the saddle. In one motion, he dropped Wolf's reins and threw himself up and left toward the pitching caboose's roof.

He found the cool, brassy rail, and he tightened his fingers, glancing down as Wolf fell back and swerved away from the thundering train. Yakima's knees slammed against the caboose's wooden panel, and he winced at the pain shooting up and down his legs.

He looked up at the rail and clenched his teeth as he drew himself toward it, the long muscles in his forearms bulging, his biceps swelling to the size of wheel hubs. The pistol barked twice more, one slug tearing into the side of the caboose while the other drilled the slack of the half-breed's right cuff.

When he got his chest above the caboose's roof, he swung his legs up and over the rail, closing his mouth as the wind sucked the air from his lungs and nearly tore his hat from his head, whipping his hair around wildly. He palmed his Colt and tugged his hat down lower on his head, looking up at the roofs of the other cars jostling to and fro under the wisping wood smoke.

"Well, you made the train . . . ," he growled uncertainly, on his hands and knees, steadying himself with the rail to his left. The wind hammered his cheeks and eyes.

Faith's captors were in the car just ahead. He'd try to get into the first car in the train's combination, then make his way back.

Yakima started forward. As he gained the vestibule between the caboose and the passenger car, he rose to his feet and glanced into the narrow gap between the cars below.

The cutthroats hadn't come out after him. He drew back, then lurched forward, easily leaping the gap between the cars and landing atop the roof of the next car, bending his knees. Crouching and holding his arms out for balance, he strode forward along the narrow iron walkway. He moved quickly, fighting the wind and balancing himself against the car's violent sway.

Below, the wheels hammered, clattering over the seams.

He was near the middle of the car when he stopped suddenly. A head rose over the car's far end, at the top of the left-side ladder. A dark, pocked face appeared, and the Mexican's lips stretched back from his teeth. He snaked an arm over the top of the car, aiming a long-barreled Remington at Yakima.

Crack!

The bullet sizzled over Yakima's head, and he dropped to a knee, quickly aiming his Colt and firing. His slug sparked and clanged off the ladder, and the half-breed pulled his head down out of sight.

Yakima looked behind.

Another head appeared over the top of the ladder at the car's other end — the big, round, balding head of a middle-aged man. He flashed a silver eyetooth, his little eyes sparking as they found Yakima, and he began snaking his own pistol over the roof.

Before the man could level his revolver, Yakima whipped around and snapped off another shot. That slug ricocheted off the riveted tin at the edge of the roof and flew wide. The older gent flinched and triggered his pistol, the slug whining an inch over Yakima's head.

Yakima fired two more shots, the first one sailing wide as the car lurched, fouling his aim. But the second slug must have torn into the big man's ear, because he howled and, jerking his head sideways, dropped straight down the ladder and out of sight.

Behind Yakima, another pistol barked, and he clamped his jaws together as the bullet burned across his right shoulder blade, tearing his shirt. He whipped around, dancing sideways, as the Mexican fired again from the car's other end, the bullet sailing off into the wind and landscape whipping past in a tan blur.

Yakima triggered a return shot, his anger and the pain in his shoulder throwing his aim off. The slug skidded off the first car farther up the swaying, rumbling line to ping off the locomotive's smokestack.

Automatically, he fired again, but the hammer clicked on an empty chamber.

He cursed. His only other weapon was the Arkansas toothpick in the sheath thonged around his neck and hanging down between his shoulder blades.

He looked up to see the Mexican grinning

as he stepped onto the roof of the passenger car, holding his gun out in his right hand. Yakima considered reaching for the toothpick, but reconsidered. The Mexican had him dead to rights.

If the man was sporting, however, Yakima might have another chance. . . .

Yakima thrust his arms forward, lifted his hands, and beckoned the man with a challenging stare. "No fun in shootin' an unarmed man, is there, amigo?"

The Mexican stood at the end of the car, balancing himself with one arm flung out and squinting down the barrel of his long-barreled Remington. He tipped his head back and sideways, and pooched out his lips, sizing up Yakima like a boxer taking an opponent's measure. He teetered back and forth with the car's sway, his long hair dancing around his homely, aggressive face.

Suddenly, he twirled the Remy on his trigger finger, dropped it into his holster, and stepped forward, squaring his shoulders and holding his hands out, palms down, drilling Yakima with his challenging, black-eyed gaze.

Yakima stepped forward in much the same pose, the smoke-laced wind swirling back from the locomotive threatening to throw him to either side while the car lurched and swayed beneath his moccasins. The Mex moved toward him, his grin widening as he thrilled to the fight, showing a devil's mouth of rotten, twisted, tobacco-stained teeth.

He opened his raised hands slightly, flung his right toward Yakima, then pulled it back and fired his left. The punch landed with a solid smack high on Yakima's right cheek, and Yakima delivered the same to the Mex, whose eyes snapped wide with surprise as he stumbled back.

He staggered too far right, and, with the car lurching this way and that, he put his left foot down quickly to keep from going over the side. As he did, Yakima stormed forward and landed a savage haymaker on the man's jaw and followed it up with a solid left that laid the man's eyebrow open like a swipe from a butcher knife.

"Mierda!" the Mex screamed as he fell hard and hit the car's roof on his back, the back of his head slamming down with a ring.

A killing fury burning through him, Yakima didn't give the Mex a chance to gather his wits much less rise before he slammed a knee onto the man's chest. The man blinked, terror glistening now in his eyes, as Yakima hammered first a right cross to his face, then a left, both blows landing solidly.

He swung his right fist back once more.

Before he could ram it forward, the Mex bucked up suddenly and Yakima, caught off balance and off guard, flew sideways, hitting the top of the car on his back. As the Mex heaved himself to his feet, blood streaming down from his cut brow, Yakima rolled toward the car's left edge, then quickly regained his feet.

The Mex lunged toward him, howling. Yakima ducked. The Mex's right arm whistled over his head.

Yakima slammed his right fist against the man's chin, then jabbed the left against his nose. As the Mex staggered back toward the other side of the car, Yakima smashed his nose twice more, until he felt the flesh give beneath his fist and saw blood wash across the man's face, as though he'd been struck with a wine flask.

The man fell to the roof and rolled over the edge with a scream, reaching up with one hand to grab the lip. He caught it with his other hand, and hung there.

Inside the car below, Faith gasped as something fell down over the window on the opposite side of the aisle from her and Lowry Temple, blocking the dusky light.

"Jesus!" said one of the two salesmen near the window, running his nervous gaze across the ceiling, which most of the other passengers, hearing the footsteps and gunfire from above, were doing as well.

Chulo Garza's bloody face smeared blood against the smoke-stained glass for about two seconds before the man screamed, *"Help me!"* and dropped straight down from the window and out of sight.

Atop the car, Yakima jerked his eyes away from where the Mex had fallen as a pistol cracked to his right, the slug whining past his nose. He lurched back as another pistol popped in the other direction, the slug clanking off steel.

He leaped to one side to recover his footing, but just then the car swerved. His feet flew out from beneath him.

"Goddamnit, Freeze!" someone bellowed above the wind and rumbling wheels. "Don't shoot in my direction, ya damn tinhorn!"

Yakima rolled down the sloped, tin-covered ceiling and felt his stomach lurch into his throat as his legs fell over the side of the car. Gravity pulled at his feet, and before he knew what had happened, he was hanging by his fingers from the edge of the car, his face pressed against a window through which he could see a stout woman in a black scarf holding a baby and glaring back at him, shouting something in German.

He gritted his teeth as he pressed his fingers into the car's roof, but even as he did, they were sliding over the curved tin. He'd no sooner looked beneath him at the raised, cinder-paved rail bed racing away beneath him, than he felt nothing but air under his hands.

The graded stones shot up at him, and he landed on his right foot, the blow smacking his jaws together with an audible *clack*. Before he could get the other foot down, he flew forward, and he was rolled down the stony bank, the sharp-edged rocks biting into his back and shoulders. Mercifully fast, the stones slipped away and he was rolling down a steep, grassy bank.

"YAA-KIMAAAA!" Faith screamed out an open window.

The cry faded as the train squawked, creaked, and rumbled around a curve, the whistle blowing suddenly to abruptly snuff the echo.

As he rolled to a stop at the bottom of the bank, his head throbbing, feeling blood leaking out from under the bandage to dribble down the side of his face, the train gave a few more dwindling chugs and fell silent as it slipped into the distance.

The ground beneath him stopped quivering.

The breeze ruffled the needle grass around him.

On his back, arms spread, Yakima sucked a breath against the Apache arrows of pain shooting through his bullet-burned temple, and he lifted his head. All he saw was a dusky green sky and the dun embankment rising on his right. On his left the grass was stippled with piñons and cedars, a few mesquites.

In the far distance, a hawk screeched. The screech sounded like "Faith."

Yakima lowered his throbbing head to the grass and cursed.

CHAPTER 17

Yakima lay there in the brown grass, so frustrated that he'd let himself get thrown from the train when he'd been only a few feet from Faith, that he wanted to end it all with his Colt.

But a bullet was too good for him. He needed to get his ass up and figure out how he was going to catch up to those cutthroats and get his woman back. He didn't have time to lie here mentally licking his wounds and lamenting his bad luck and idiocy.

When he finally heaved himself up from the grass, slitting his eyes as his head barked at every breath and movement, things looked just as hopeless as they had when he was on his back. There was no sign of the town behind him. He didn't know how long he'd been on the train or how fast it had been traveling — probably fourteen or fifteen miles an hour — but he had to be at least a couple of miles from town.

Nothing to do but head back for it. He doubted there'd be another train through here for a couple of days, so he'd have to retrieve his horses and start heading cross-country. If he busted ass, he might be able to overtake the cutthroats before they gained Trinidad, at the border of Colorado and New Mexico Territory.

But he hadn't walked the rails for five minutes before the smell of blood wafted like copper on the cooling night air, and he looked around to see bits and pieces of blood-soaked clothing lying strewn between the rails like carrion left by coyotes or wolves. About ten yards farther up the track lay a severed human arm in a thick coat sleeve of bear hide. The hand was gloved.

The Mex whom Yakima had fought atop the passenger car must have gotten sucked down under the train's iron wheels.

Yakima had smelled fresh blood before, but in his current state — defeated both physically and mentally — his gut heaved, his vision swam, and his moccasins turned to lead.

He staggered down off the graded rail bed and looked around for a place to hole up for the night. There was no point in going on. He'd likely pass out before he made it back to the depot town. He might as well hole up, get some sheltered rest, and start fresh in the morning.

Stumbling around in the thickening darkness, he found an arroyo concealed in mesquites and spindly desert berry shrubs. He reloaded his Colt from his shell belt before he dropped down into the cut — a rocky gorge littered with flood debris and dead leaves.

There were several notch caves at the base of the steep walls, and, finding one large enough to conceal him from a possible rainstorm and Apaches, he poked a stick in it to make sure a bobcat wasn't calling it home, then brushed out the large rocks and rabbit shit.

He gathered some small chunks of wood and built a fire where the cut's overhanging willow shrubs would conceal the smoke, then sat down heavily and rested his back against the ravine wall.

"Shit."

He didn't usually imbibe in liquor stronger than beer except for medicinal purposes, but he could have used a stiff shot of rye. But there was no rye. Not even any water. He probably could have found a spring if he looked around, but the darkness was washing quickly down from the Mogollons in the south. He'd sit tight and roll a smoke and try to get a couple of winks before resuming his tramp to town.

He smoked the cigarette while leaning against the ravine wall, the small, crackling fire holding the desert chill at bay. Staring at the stars, he tried to count the constellations to keep his mind from Faith and the distance that was, every second he sat here smoking his cigarette and staring at the stars, growing between them.

He didn't know that he'd slept before his own grunt woke him.

Lifting his head from his shoulder, he looked around. Soft gray light had seeped into the arroyo. The moon must have come up. But he raked his gaze across the sky in which the stars had faded, and he couldn't see one.

He looked at his fire. Nothing but gray ashes with a few bits of blackened wood sticking out. His quirley lay on the ground beside his right hand, a good three inches of gray ash snaking up from the flat, slightly chewed butt. The ash was as insubstantial as a spider's web, and as cold as the ground.

He looked around once more, his neck muscles feeling as though they'd turned to rawhide. Blood had crusted on the side of his head, where it had run down from the bandage. Birds were chirping in the brush, and the dense night chill was lifting.

Christ, he'd slept all night. It was damn near dawn.

He kicked to his feet, a scowl biting deep into his forehead, and, donning his hat, scrambled back out of the arroyo. Getting his bearings, he headed back to the rails and began walking, sort of half skipping the inconveniently spaced ties, toward the town of unknown name in the west.

He should have retrieved his horses and been heading east by now. But he had to admit that the sleep had done him good. It had lightened the throb in his head and generally rejuvenated him in spite of the lingering stiffness not only from the fight and the tumble from the car's roof, but from the several hours he'd slept in the chill arroyo, his back against the cool, uneven bank.

He'd walked about a hundred yards beyond the Mexican's strewn remains, much of which appeared to have been dragged off by a bobcat during the night, when he stopped and lifted his chin, frowning along the rails ahead of him. The sun was a pearl wash behind him, and the rails were two brown, silver-mottled snakes stretching west. Above the distant black ridges, several stars still guttered in a lilac sky.

He'd heard something. He'd spied movement in the dense shadows straight ahead.

It came again — a *chug.*

A bell clanged, and there was another *chug,* and Yakima felt the stiff muscles in his neck suddenly loosen.

A train!

He quickened his pace, awkwardly skipping the ties, and watched the bulky silhouette of the snub-nosed locomotive grow before him. The rumble of iron wheels and the pant of compressors sounded disturbingly like the primal beats of an Apache war dance, but his heart beat eagerly.

He couldn't have been happier to run into another train heading west. He'd leave the horses and acquire some strong runners when he needed them farther on up the line — probably in Denver.

The train came on quickly, squawking and squealing and rumbling, the locomotive snorting like a giant bull buffalo in heat, and Yakima could feel the vibration intensifying beneath his moccasins. When the train was about seventy yards away, the night lanterns jostling and flashing on both sides of the cowcatcher, he scrambled down the raised bed where he could get a good look at the combination and figure which car to run for.

The train came fast, smoke pluming from its stack, cinders flashing like fireflies. But behind it, instead of the eight or nine cars Yakima was expecting to see, was only a tender car heaped with wood, a flatbed, and what appeared from this distance to be a slat-sided stock car.

"Hell . . ."

"Yakima!" a familiar voice shouted. "That you?"

A bell in the engine clanged, and there was the inexplicable sound of breaking glass nearly drowned by the locomotive's chugging thunder. Just as inexplicably, there was a wind-torn whinny of a horse.

Instinctively, Yakima's hand dropped to his Colt's grips, but he left the revolver in its holster as he said, so softly that even he could barely hear, "Who the hell . . . ?"

"Come on, ya bloody redskin!" the familiar voice shouted once more as a hand waved outside the engine's window. "Don't stand there gawkin' like you never seen an iron mustang before! Come and join the bloody party before these Irish drink all the hooch!"

"Harms?" Yakima muttered, incredulous.

The train approached, bell clanging and whistle blowing, an Irish-accented voice singing inside the engine's cab. Brody

Harms, poking his bespectacled head out from the vestibule, beckoned broadly.

"Run!"

"I'll be damned," Yakima grunted, breaking into a run.

He scrambled up the rocky bed and gained the crest just as the big double 00s on the engine's nose drew even with him. Throwing up his right arm, he saw Brody Harms grinning, the Easterner's spectacles colored with milky dawn light as he leaned so far out of the engine's vestibule that he was nearly perpendicular to the ground.

Harms's hand slapped Yakima's. At the same time, Yakima lurched toward the vestibule, grabbed the brass rail with his free hand, and let Harms heave him toward the engine with a powerful pull. He got his right foot on the bottom step, and Harms backed up the other two steps, pulling Yakima's arm.

The two fell together on the engine's cold steel floor. Yakima looked up at the Easterner lying on his side beside him, then beyond him at the other two men in the engine's tight quarters.

A beefy gent with thick, strawberry blond hair and matching mustache was sitting in the iron swivel chair, manning the controls. The other, compact and wiry, with a face that looked as though it had been hacked apart by Comanches, then sewn together with catgut, sat by the near wall opposite the roaring broiler, beneath the wood-handled rope dangling from a bell.

He had a bottle in his gloved hand. The bottle was resting against his thigh clad in pin-striped overalls. Smiling drunkenly at Yakima, he pooched out his thick lips, raised the bottle in salute, then tipped it back. Whiskey dribbled out from around the bottle to stream down his knobby chin and prominent Adam's apple.

Yakima dropped his gaze to Harms, still grinning beside him. "What's all this?"

"That's Steve at the controls. This here's Bob. Met 'em in Salida." He lifted his chin toward the tender car rocking and rattling behind the engine. "This is their baby," the Easterner added, reaching back to pound the iron bulkhead. "Repair crew. They'd been workin' for the Santa Fe line for nearly twelve years, until two days ago."

"Drinkin' on the job!" Steve shouted, not looking at Yakima but ducking his head to put his face up against a pressure gauge.

"Not only drinkin'," Bob said, offering the bottle to Yakima, who grabbed it around the neck. "But we decided to bring a couple of whores along, to keep us company while we were repairing a bridge down south of Coyotero Gulch. It gets cold up there of an evenin', don't ya know. The super got wind of it and fired us outright."

"After five years!" Steve shouted, leaning forward to stare out the window, his pinstriped engineer's cap tipped back on his freckled head. "As though he'd never broken the rules. Bullshit! I've seen him with my own eyes" — he turned awkwardly toward Yakima and, as though there were some question about whose eyes he'd see it with, pointed at his watery blues with a gloved index and forefinger — "with buck-naked cleaning girls bent over his desk!"

Yakima turned to Harms, whose breath smelled like a vat of saloon-brewed busthead. "I thought I heard Wolf's whinny."

"We hitched up a stock car. Wolf and the three Indian ponies." Harms squinted one brown eye behind his spectacles. "You know how hard it was to load three *Apache* ponies onto a train car? They screamed like we were dousing their mangy hides with kerosene."

"The constable heard it," Bob put in, though his words were so garbled that it took Yakima a second to translate. "Him and Turner — that's the ramrod — come runnin' as we were pullin' out of the train yard.

Course, they might have heard us fire up the boiler, too." He grinned like the cat that ate the canary, showing two rows of large white teeth. "Probably got a posse out after us. They'll never catch us. We got this thing so hopped up on pine and cottonwood, they'd need to sprout wings to run us down. And there ain't no more locomotives for a good sixty miles in any direction."

"Free as the friggin' wind!" Steve shouted, holding up his arm in a victory salute and blowing the horn. "Piss on the Atchison, Topeka, and Santa Fe!" His words were nearly lost beneath the blast, which was so shrill as it echoed around the bulkheads that Yakima thought his brains were going to dribble out his ears.

"Piss on it!" Bob agreed. "And piss on George Turner!"

Harms yelled in Yakima's ear. "I think that, if I hadn't talked them into stealing a train for me, they would have shot their former employer. So I guess you could say I'm saving them from a hang rope!"

Yakima was incredulous. "You mean to tell me they're doing this just to get even with their boss?"

"That and" — Harms plucked a small, round burlap pouch from a boot well and hefted it in his hand — "and a half shot

223

glass each of gold dust. They intend to buy themselves a little cantina somewhere in Mexico and start living the good life."

"I'll be damned," Yakima said, staring at the pouch in Harms's work-calloused hand. "You finally hit a vein."

"Two weeks ago."

Yakima laughed. "Christ! I'll pay ya back . . . somehow."

Harms returned the pouch to his boot. "No need." He clamped a hand over Yakima's shoulder, his head wobbling, eyes looking slightly out of focus. Tears squeezed out from under his glasses, and his voiced thickened with drunken sentiment. "It's for you and Faith, you mangy redskin."

Yakima laid his own gloved hand over the inebriated Easterner's right ear and gave Harms's head an affectionate shake. "Obliged."

On the other side of Harms, Bob yelled, "You ain't gonna hog the bottle, now, are ya?"

Yakima glanced at the bottle in his hand, from which he hadn't yet drunk. He tipped back a liberal pull, enjoying the near instantaneous abatement of his aches and pains, then offered the bottle to Harms. Brody waved it off, shaking his head, as if to say he'd had his fill.

Yakima gave the bottle back to Bob, who held it up, squinting to check the level, then took several swallows before passing it on to Steve. The bottle went around a couple more times before Yakima had had his fill for medicinal purposes.

Brody Harms said, "Think I'll go take a little snooze," and climbed up into the tender car to snuggle down atop the wood.

"Think I'll join ya," Bob said, rising by pushing his shoulders against the bulkhead behind him with his feet. Then he staggered on out the back of the engine and climbed into the tender car behind Harms.

Yakima got up to look out the locomotive's open left-side window, seeing little but rolling desert slowly lightening as the sun rose. He moved up to the left of Steve to peer over the Baldwin's long, rusting nose and around the diamond-shaped stack.

Straight ahead, the red-orange sun peeked out from between distant ridges silhouetted against it.

"Where the hell are we?" he yelled above the chugging din, squinting as a black smoke plume brushed through the window to sting his eyes with hot soot.

Steve said nothing. Yakima turned toward him, opening his mouth to repeat the question, but closed it.

The engineer had passed out, his ruddy, freckled face pressed up against the cab's front window. His mouth was open, and drool dribbled down over his bottom lip.

Yakima looked around anxiously, as if someone else capable of driving the train might be hidden somewhere in the cramped, smoky cab. He jerked Steve's shoulder. "Hey, wake up, there, partner!"

It didn't take much prodding to realize that Steve was out cold, and, judging by the stench of his breath, he'd be out a good, long time.

"Ah, hell!" Yakima grunted, throwing the man's arm around his neck and pulling him off the stool. He eased him down against the bulkhead where Bob had been sitting.

Straightening, Yakima flicked his wary eyes around the cab, nervously rubbing his palms on his thighs. He was a good ten hours behind Faith, barreling through western New Mexico Territory on an ancient, rickety work train that no longer had a pilot. He had not only never driven a locomotive before, but he'd never, until now, been in the cab of one.

From the rear of the train, a whinny rose, swirling on the wind, and was nearly drowned by the train's clatter. Yakima would have recognized Wolf's skeptical bugling anywhere.

How did the beast always know when they were in trouble?

"Shut up, ya old cayuse," Yakima muttered, raking his eyes across what seemed a good three dozen dials, levers, and knobs jutting from the bulkheads all around him, and then at the boiler's dirty iron door.

He bit his cheek, then leaned down to scrutinize the dials and gauges, and gently probed a lever with an index finger. Uncertainly, he said, rubbing a sleeve over a glass dial, "I'll get the hang of it in no time."

CHAPTER 18

You can usually get the hang of anything when you're placed between doing so and the bores of a double-barreled, ten-gauge shotgun with its hammers eared back.

And that in a sense was where Yakima was, with the work train's two pilots having been rendered comatose by tanglefoot, and with him needing to make up precious time if he was going to keep Faith from falling into the hands of Bill Thornton in Colorado Territory.

He could only hope that he wasn't going to wreck the train by blowing its boiler or running it off the track.

He quickly found out that keeping the rumbling, clamoring contraption on the rails and adjusting its speed, slowing for downgrades and turns and increasing for upgrades and long, flat stretches, was accomplished by a couple of levers and a round porcelain knob. The hard part was keeping the boilers stoked without letting a couple of needles leap into the red areas of their dials — in other words, without over-heating the water in the locomotive's huge belly boiler and threatening to blow himself and his passengers and horses into instant viscera and spreading them across ten square miles of New Mexico Territory.

He'd seen the result of boiler explosions before, when he'd been laying track for the Southern Pacific, and he never wanted to see such a twisted concoction of scalded wreckage and carnage again, much less become part of it.

At about noon of that day, when he felt he had a relative handle on the locomotive's workings and had just finished stoking its boiler for the fourth time, he found a map in a cubbyhole under the front window, and leaned back in the pilot's chair to smoke a quirley and study it.

According to the map this line of track dipped a good distance south before joining up with the north–south line in Belen, New Mexico Territory. That being so, the only way Yakima and Harms could make up time on Faith's kidnappers was to disembark the train before the southern dip.

Riding hard and switching horses often, they'd sprint northeast for the Colorado border. The rail line the kidnappers would take to Denver curved sharply into eastern Colorado, with a couple more connections, before jogging back west and north to the city itself. If Yakima and Harms could make a beeline for Denver — or as much of a beeline as possible in this mountainous terrain — they might be able to reach it at about the same time the kidnappers did, and cut them off before they could light out for Thornton's place farther north and west.

He lowered the map, inhaled a lungful of tobacco smoke, and squinted out across the sun-washed, cedar-tufted hills rumpling before him, making some quick mental calculations. Faith's group would probably arrive in Denver in about two and a half days.

Yakima and Harms would have to push hard, but avoiding unforeseen obstacles and problems with the horses, it could be done.

He field-stripped the quirley, let the wind take it, then scrutinized the dials before retrieving wood from the tender car and stoking the boiler stove once more. He stood up near the pilot's chair and watched the terrain fold, roll, and unfold slowly around him as the rattling train climbed hills between fir- and aspen-carpeted slopes, dropped into vast, devil's playgrounds of red-rock canyons, and stretched out across yucca- and cedar-stippled plains under a clear, dry Southwestern sky.

Cloud shadows danced across the coppery terrain.

Deer grazed foothills, and hawks lazed on high thermals. A couple of times he spied Indian hunting parties — probably Navajo — riding in small clumps on spotted ponies along a distant, buckskin-colored slope or meandering over a pine-carpeted ridge, their dark, feather-limned heads bowed to study the terrain below them.

Mentally, Yakima pulled the miles back behind him, frustrated by the train's slow progress and frustrated further by having been so close to getting Faith back only a few hours ago. He'd nearly had her.

Around four o'clock that afternoon, with the sun angling down behind him and the country ahead bleeding shadows, he pulled down hard on the brake levers, then braced himself as the engine's floor lurched beneath him. He fell up against the cab's front panel but continued pulling down on the levers until the train had bucked, screeched, and chugged to a stop not far from a tin water tank on a high wooden pedestal.

They were in a shade-dappled valley strewn with boulders and spinelike stone ridges. Far ahead, down a gradual hill and just north of where the rails made their long, slow swing south around a distant mountain range, a village appeared — white adobe hovels and corrals nestled in sage and bordered on one side by a brush-sheathed stream.

Yakima grabbed his hat off the lever he'd snagged it on, then leaped down from the engine and began tramping back along the gravel-paved grade toward the stock car at the rear. The horses clomped and whinnied, bouncing the car as though it were still moving.

"Where the hell are we?" came a garbled cry from the flatcar behind the wood tender.

Yakima turned to see Bob, Steve, and Brody Harms sitting up from where they'd obviously been napping amongst the strapped-down crates and barrels sprouting picks, shovels, bars, and sundry other track-repair equipment. All three looked as though they'd just been awakened from graves in which they'd been moldering for fifty years.

"End of the line," Yakima said, continuing on past the men toward the flatcar. "At least *our* line."

He leaped onto the narrow ledge running along the side of the stock car and gave one of the doors a tug. He glanced back toward the flatbed from which Harms was easing himself down, placing his bowler ever-so-gently on his head, as though it were a crown of thorns.

The other two were still looking around blinking through the mussed hair in their eyes. Bob reached blindly around for a nearby bottle while Steve lay back against a burlap sack, hacking phlegm from his throat.

"I *no comprende*," Harms said, wincing as he pulled his hands slowly away from his hat. "I thought we met up with the north–south line in Belen."

"We would." Yakima drew the other door open and was met with Wolf's eager, bugling whinny. "But we're takin' a shortcut." He turned to step into the stock car, then stopped suddenly and swung back around to Harms. "If you're still in, that is. There's only three of those sons o' bitches left, and I reckon I can handle 'em if you wanna go on home. You look like you just throwed down from the moon."

Judging by the Easterner's pain-stretched lips and bloodshot eyes, his head must have felt like a barrel-sized, open wound. The hard ride they were facing might kill him . . . or make him wish he were dead.

"Ah, shut up," he grouched, leaping up onto the stock car and doing his best to pretend the maneuver didn't feel like a war club to his head. "You're preachier than my old Presbyterian pastor. Why don't you quit yackin' so we can saddle these horses and get after your woman?"

When Yakima and his hungover Eastern friend had led their four fiddle-footing mounts down the stock car's wooden ramp and rigged them up, they swung into their saddles and rode up to where Bob and Steve sat with their legs hanging down over the edge of the flat car, passing the bottle between them.

"Hair of the dog?" Steve said, raising the half-empty bottle, his big yellow teeth showing beneath his thick red mustache.

"Don't mind if I do."

Harms gigged his horse up to the car and reached down for the whiskey. When he'd taken a swig, he offered it to Yakima, who shook his head. The Easterner took another, smaller pull, then gave the bottle back to Steve.

"That should deaden the pain for the first few miles, anyway." Harms looked at Steve and Bob. "You boys best head down to the village yonder, buy yourselves a couple of good horses and hightail it to Mexico. The railroad will no doubt be along for their work train."

"Ha!" Bob howled, slapping his thigh. "Mexico, here we come!"

Yakima pinched his hat brim to the two men, who'd resumed their dog-hair imbibing with the fervor of Irish track layers on their first trip to San Francisco. "Obliged for the ride!" he called over his shoulder as he jogged Wolf and the trailing Apache pony up beside the locomotive.

He turned the horses around the cowcatcher, then down the other side of the grade and up through the rocky, sparsely pine-stippled valley, angling northwest.

During that first hour of hard riding, he glanced behind a couple times, surprised to see Brody Harms staying close off the Apache pony's bushy tail. The hungover prospector fell behind after dark, but never so far that Yakima didn't hear his hoof thuds. Once, when they'd stopped to water the horses at a run-out spring in the foothills of a vast range humping up blackly in the east, he heard Harms retching off in the shrubs.

"You all right?" Yakima asked the man as he stumbled back toward the half-breed and the horses, wiping his mouth with a red handkerchief.

"Peachy," Harms said as he swung back

into his saddle.

They switched horses around nine o'clock that night, and continued riding until after midnight. As the terrain had grown rougher the farther they'd angled northwest toward Trinidad on the Colorado–New Mexico border, they stopped for a brief rest about three o'clock in the morning.

They threw down some jerky and biscuits that Harms had picked up in the rail town of Salida, and shrugged into their cold-weather gear. They were gaining elevation, and frost limned the piñons and lodgepole pines, and their breath puffed in the chill air, glinting in the starlight.

Later that night they rode onto a cougar feeding on a deer, and both men fired several shots as the cat chased them through a shallow canyon. They were riding too fast for accurate shooting, but they must have discouraged their feline stalker, for the savage snarls soon faded after they left the arroyo.

A half hour later they felt safe enough to sheathe their rifles and to turn their attention to the vague horse trail ahead of them.

Noon of the next day found them jogging along the broad main street of a little town perched on a high, windy plain under a mass of low, snow-spitting clouds. Evidently the place had once been a Mexican pueblito. There was a grim-looking adobe church at the far end, but the Mexican mud huts had long since been outnumbered by two- and three-story, false-fronted business buildings constructed of whipsawed pine boards. They stood tall along both sides of the wide street in which frozen mud puddles wore a dusting of new snow.

The town looked deserted except for a few stock ponies tied about halfway down the left side of the street. They fronted a saloon called Lucky Joe's from which soft piano music emanated, as did a woman's screeching, raucous laughter. A brick chimney crawling up the building's far side fed gray smoke to the steely sky, tingeing the brittle air with the spicy, succulent smell of chili.

"Might as well rest the horses for a couple of hours," Yakima said, angling toward the hitch rail. He didn't want to stop, but killing the horses as well as themselves would get them nowhere. Besides, they were making good time and were likely halfway to Denver. There'd be no point arriving ahead of the train. "Let's pad our bellies and get a drink."

"Didn't I tell you?" Harms said behind the scarf he'd wrapped around his mouth. "I've sworn off liquor. Yessir, riding with you and a hangover did away with the whole notion. I may even rejoin the church!"

"Get yourself a God-fearin' woman?"

"Don't push it."

Yakima gave a wry snort as he looped his horses' reins around the hitch rail. Wolf had nothing but disdain for the Indian ponies, and the feeling was mutual, so the half-breed tied the horses a good distance apart.

As Wolf and the Apache mounts shared evil sidelong glances, heads up and snorting despite their trail fatigue, he loosened Wolf's saddle cinch and slipped his bridle bit so the horse could drink freely at the stock tank flanking the hitch rail.

A jellied layer of ice had formed on the water's surface. Yakima stirred the straw-flecked black water around with a stick, then joined Brody Harms on the saloon's front porch. Both men glanced at the sky hovering low over the town's rooftops, wood smoke skeining from brick chimneys as small granular flakes continued to fall.

"Well, it's winter," Yakima said with a resigned air, lowering the collar of his jaguar coat and stamping snow from his moccasin boots. "We could run into more of this the farther we head north, so we best be prepared for it." As he turned toward the saloon, he added, "We'll lay in some grain before we head out again."

He tripped the latch of the saloon's glass-topped door, in which LUCKY JOE'S had been printed in green gold-leaf lettering adorned with grinning leprechauns, and moved on into the saloon, spurs chinking over the puncheons as Harms moved in behind him.

The woman was laughing again, and as Harms closed the door, Yakima removed his hat to sweep snow from the brim. Then he tramped toward the bar running along the deep, low-ceilinged room's right wall.

As he did, he raked his eyes around, noting the eight men in drover's garb sitting at two tables to the left of the bar. An enormously fat, round-faced woman in a scanty gown and wolf shawl was perched heavily atop the knee of a red-faced gent with long blond hair, her stout arms wrapped around the man's thick neck. As her head turned toward Yakima — as all the heads in the room did — her laughter stopped abruptly, and a frown dug into her painted forehead.

"What do we have here?" Yakima heard the woman mutter as he stepped up to the bar.

A tall, lanky gent had been placing bottles on the high shelves of the back bar. Now, as the room fell silent behind him, he glanced toward the door over his right shoulder, his pale blue eyes flicking between Yakima and Harms while acquiring a troubled cast.

"Uh, take note of the sign," he said, turning full around and pointing with the corked bottle in his fist. Long, thick gray hair hung to his shoulders, and he spoke in a faint Irish accent.

Yakima glanced at a chalkboard nailed to a ceiling joist to his left. On the board the silhouette of an Indian head had been chalked, complete with hawkish nose and feathered headdress. A large X was slashed across the figure and, as though for emphasis, NO INJUNS had been scrawled in poor penmanship below.

The bartender, who wore an open fur coat over a bloodstained apron, sneered. "Drew a picture for those who can't read."

He smiled at Yakima.

Harms glanced at his partner and winced. "Oh dear."

CHAPTER 19

Yakima stared across the bar at the Irish apron, his face implacable. But his chest was burning. Before he could reach across the bar to grab the man by his shirt, Brody Harms stepped up beside him.

"That's ridiculous," the Easterner said with a dry laugh. "Can't you see Yakima's green eyes? He probably has as much white blood as you do, my friend!"

From a nearby table, someone growled into the silence, which was relieved only by the crackling, sighing woodstove, "Half-breeds is even worse."

The woman chuckled.

The burn in Yakima's chest grew, and his jaws were set so hard they ached. He didn't want to cause trouble. Faith needed him. But the old fury at being treated like a mongrel cur that had wandered in out of the brush was one he couldn't deny.

His Colt was in his hand before he could

stop himself, bucking and roaring.

The slugs shattered first one bottle standing on a beer keg behind the bar, and then the other bottle standing beside it. Glass and liquor flew against the back bar cabinet. Shards crashed onto the floor.

Dust sifted from the rafters, and smoke wafted.

"Jesus Christ!" someone behind Yakima trilled.

Chairs squawked and groaned as the sitters jerked their attentions to the bar.

The bartender had bounded back to one side, raising his hands defensively. Now he swung his head from the broken bottles and the two bullet holes in the cabinet behind them, to Yakima, his broad, broken-nosed face flushed with fury.

"Just who in the hell do you think — ?"

"He's just a man wanting a drink and a bowl of chili, partner," Harms said as Yakima stared across the bar at the apron, his revolver cocked and ready to cut loose once more — this time at the apron's head. "Make it two of each." He sighed and looked at Yakima. "I'm drinking again."

The barman's glance flicked between Yakima and Harms.

Muttering rose from behind. Someone chuckled softly. The woman said, just as softly, "Dirty savage . . ."

The barman's face softened slightly, his eyes apprehensive. He snarled a curse, then grabbed two shot glasses off a pyramid atop the bar, and filled each with whiskey. He slid the drinks in front of Yakima and Harms, then walked down to where a smoking, grease-splattered iron range sat against the back wall.

He ladled two bowls of chili from a black pot, set those too before the newcomers, then rattled spoons down beside the bowls. Crossing his arms on his broad chest, he fixed Yakima with a belligerent stare. "That'll be two dollars. I don't barter or extend credit to . . . strangers."

Yakima twirled his Colt on his finger, dropped it into his holster, then reached into his jeans pocket. When he'd tossed a few coins onto the counter, he picked up his shot glass, poked his hat back off his bandaged forehead, and sipped. Ignoring the barman still glaring down at him and the stares of the others burning into his back, he leaned forward, picked up his spoon, and began casually eating the chili.

When he'd taken a couple bites, he glanced to his right. Harms stood looking across his shoulder at the men and the woman at the tables, a look of consternation on his bespectacled face.

Yakima reached over and flicked the man's spoon into the air. It hit the bar top with a clatter that made Harms jump with a start and turn his gaze back to Yakima.

"Eat up," the half-breed said, glancing briefly at the barman still glaring down at him with his arms crossed on his chest. "He ain't much for manners, but his chili ain't half bad."

Harms made a nervous face, then, glancing once more at the tables, leaned forward and spooned up some chili. When he'd eaten a couple of bites, he threw back his entire whiskey shot and slid the empty glass toward the bartender. "Refill that for me, will you?"

When, chuffing angrily, the barman had refilled the shot glass, Harms took a small sip, then resumed eating. Yakima could sense the Easterner was nervous. He, too, was edgy, though he continued to eat the chili and take small sips from his whiskey as though it were a lazy Sunday noon and he had all day to enjoy his meal.

He detected barely audible whispers behind him; then someone grunted and several chairs scraped across the puncheons. Harms turned his head to look over his shoulder again as Yakima kept his head tipped over his chili bowl. But in the corner of his left eye, he watched three men rise from their chairs and, moving around the near table, saunter up toward Yakima and Harms, their thumbs hooked behind their shell belts.

"Ah, shit," Harms sighed, dropping his spoon into his half-empty chili bowl. "I feel a bad case of heartburn coming on."

Yakima swallowed a mouthful of chili, washed it down with the whiskey, then glanced over his shoulder. He arched a brow, as though surprised to see the three men — a big man and two others a couple inches shorter than Yakima — standing behind him, heads canted back on their shoulders, challenging looks on their hard, weathered faces.

Yakima turned full around. As he did, he shoved Harms off down toward the end of the bar with his left hand. Harms stepped away, stopped to grab his chili bowl and his shot glass, then continued scuffing back along the bar, his wary gaze on the three men facing Yakima.

Yakima rested his elbows on the bar top as he blandly regarded the three — the big man in the middle, the shorter gents to each side. The big man had a rectangular head with wide-spaced dark eyes, a handlebar mustache, and a lantern jaw. He wore a sheepskin vest and no hat. His thick, wavy, salt-and-pepper hair hung down over his ears.

The man on the left — a pale, blue-eyed gent with a broad-brimmed black hat decorated with silver conchos — wore woolly chaps and an old Colt Navy revolver positioned for the cross draw on his left hip. A whiskey-damp mustache drooped down over both sides of his mouth.

The man to Yakima's right wore his long, frizzy red hair parted on one side. He had a matching soup-strainer mustache and opaque gray eyes, one pale lid pulled down low beneath a knotted scar. A necklace of wolf teeth hung from a thong over his bullhide, fleece-lined vest that was as scratched and cracked as a desert playa.

He, too, wore a Colt Navy while the big man in the group's middle wore two big bowie knives on his hips, with a Colt .45 angled over his belly.

The pale gent on the left angled his head toward the chalkboard. "That rule is townwide. It ain't just Finnegan's."

Yakima returned his stare, expressionless, leaning back on his elbows.

"That means you're breakin' a town ordinance, breed," said the gent with frizzy

246

red hair. His mustache was so thick his lips didn't appear to move when he talked. "Me an' Skip and Sundance work for the town marshal on weekends and holidays. So when we tell you to get your red ass outta here, it's the law talkin', not just a passel of range riders who don't like Injuns — mixed breeds or otherwise."

"Even though we don't," added the cowboy who Yakima assumed was Sundance.

Skip hadn't yet said anything, but just stood glowering at Yakima from his full six feet five inches, a cruel smile pulling at his mouth corners, thumbs hooked behind his cartridge belt.

"I'll take that under consideration," Yakima grunted. "Now suppose you fellas take your gorilla and go back and sit down so I can finish my chili. As soon as I'm done, I'll vamoose." He hardened his eyes but tried to keep his rage on a short leash. "But not before I've eaten my chili."

He started to turn back toward the bar.

Skip reached toward Yakima's shoulder. "Who you callin' gorilla, Red — ?"

Wheeling back suddenly, Yakima sank his right fist liver-deep into Skip's solar plexus, so that the last syllable of "Redskin" burst from the big man's lips as a sort of "Skawh-hhh!" as he doubled over and drew both his thick arms across his gut.

As the man staggered back, head down, Yakima snapped his right knee up against his forehead. The man's head jerked up, and he stumbled straight back, bellowing like a poleaxed bull.

At the same time, the redheaded cowboy reached for his Colt, but his hand had barely touched the walnut grips before Yakima, jumping up and wheeling two feet above the floor, smashed his right heel against the side of the man's face.

The connection made a crunching *smack.*

Screaming, the red-haired gent flew sideways across a vacant table, his lower jaw hanging askew.

Yakima turned left, ready to parry a blow from Sundance. Brody Harms smashed his own right hand down on the hand Sundance was using to raise his Colt Navy toward Yakima.

The man cursed as the gun hit the floor, the revolver roaring and the slug thumping into the ceiling. Harms rammed his left fist against the back of Sundance's head, then his right against his forehead, dropping him in his tracks.

Sundance raised both hands to his head, shouting, "Goddamn *sons o' bitches!*"

Yakima wheeled back the other way, raking his eyes between the barman, who stood red faced and mute behind the bar, pooching out his thick lips with disgust, and the five other cowboys and the whore at the other table about twenty feet away.

One of the men was frozen half out of his chair, hand on his gun, regarding Yakima from beneath shaggy salt-and-pepper brows.

Yakima stared at him hard and the man melted like butter back down into his chair, raising his hands casually above the table, where he picked up a card deck but kept his hate-filled eyes on Yakima. The others stared at him as well, angry and wary.

The whore looked scared — glassy eyed, red faced, and holding her shawl across her enormous breasts, as though she'd suddenly found herself in the presence of a wounded bobcat.

Yakima glanced at Harms. The Easterner stood over Sundance, who was still down and rolling around in pain, cursing.

"Nice one. Grab his gun."

As Harms reached down to disarm Sundance, Yakima walked over to pluck the Colt from the red-haired cowboy's holster. The man lay on the floor with his head propped against a ceiling joist. He probed his swelling jaw with both hands, groaning, his mouth sounding as though he were chomping on jawbreakers.

"You . . . you broke my jaw, you bastard."

Yakima tossed his Colt into a far corner, then walked over to Skip. The big man was on his hands and knees, bellowing, "God-damnit!" over and over through bloody hands clamped over his nose.

Yakima placed his moccasin boot between the man's shoulder blades and kicked him belly down against the floor. Then he removed Skip's knives from his hip holsters and tossed them into a corner. He kicked the man over onto his back, delivering another savage blow to his ribs, and pulled the Colt .45 from Skip's belly holster. He tossed the gun into the corner with the knives.

Drawing his Colt from its holster, and cocking the hammer, Yakima backed toward the bar. "I'm amending the rule a bit. In-juns are now allowed, but assholes are hereby banned from the premises." He popped a shot into the puncheons between Skip and Sundance. "All three of you ass-holes — *out!*"

The red-haired gent, words bizarrely garbled, told Yakima to diddle his mother. At least, that's what it sounded like through the jawbreakers.

Yakima drilled a bullet into the ceiling

joist above the cowboy's head. The man jerked with a curse, wide-eyed with horror, and began heaving himself to his feet.

Sundance and Skip did likewise, and as Yakima held his cocked Colt on them, keeping one eye skinned on the bartender and on the other men in the room, they made their way to the door. Like the walking wounded of a long, pitched battle, they stumbled outside and across the porch, groaning and cursing, their boots scuffing and thudding, leaving the door standing wide behind them.

Brody Harms went over and closed the door, then turned to look at Yakima anxiously.

Yakima set his revolver on the bar and turned to his chili. He took a bite, set his spoon down, shoved his bowl forward, and looked at the bartender. "Food's cold. Throw in some hot. Refill my partner's bowl, too. We have a long ride ahead."

Grumbling, the bartender did as he was told. As the other customers and the whore spoke in hushed tones off Yakima's left flank, Brody Harms pressed his back to the bar beside him and said in a conspiratorial tone, "Shouldn't we, uh, maybe light on out of here?"

Yakima's fury was still a wildfire in his

belly. He knew a good deal of his anger was caused by shot nerves over Faith, but he'd never taken to being treated like a mangy dog, and, the world be damned, he'd go down fighting such treatment like a gut-shot wolverine.

"So soon?" He poured his friend a fresh drink from the bottle before him. "We just got here."

CHAPTER 20

In his roadhouse in northern Colorado, Bill
Thornton awoke with a start, jerking his
head up from his pillow, his heart racing.

"What is it?"

Blinking the sleep from his eyes, he turned
to the Indian whore, Ruby, sitting up in bed
beside him, frowning over the nail file in
her hand.

"Didn't you hear it?"

"Hear what?"

Thornton stared at the red and gold-
papered wall beyond the bed, to the left of
the closed hall door, and pricked his ears,
listening. There was only the late-autumn
wind rustling leaves in the yard and whining under the eaves, the squawk and muffled
thud of an outbuilding door slapping free
against its frame.

He turned to the window. Wan gray light
pushed through the dusty panes.

"It was only me." Ruby ran her nail file

over her fingers quickly, and stopped. "Filing my nails, huh?"

Thornton let out a held breath. "I reckon. Thought I heard voices. Must have just been dreaming they were bringing that bitch back to me."

Ruby ran the file across her nails again, then stopped. "Bitch?"

"Faith."

"You don't need her." Ruby pulled the buffalo robe down to her waist, exposing her full, olive-colored breasts with their brown nipples, and slumped toward him, letting her breasts slope toward his sweat-beaded face, giving him a good look. "See? You don't need her. You got Ruby."

Thornton chuckled and cupped the girl's right breast in his hand. "You got that right. No need to be jealous, Ruby. I ain't havin' that bitch hauled back here to take your place. I'm havin' her hauled back here so I can punish her the way she deserves to be punished."

He closed his hand over the girl's breast and hardened his jaws. "The way a whore oughta be punished, who did to me what that whore did!"

"Oww!" Ruby complained, tensing suddenly.

Thornton looked up at the girl scowling

down at him, her dark cheeks flushed, eyes etched with pain. He'd squeezed her too hard. Pulling his hand away from the red-mottled breast, he turned away, his face warming with chagrin.

"You too rough, sometimes, Bill!" Rubbing her breast, the girl scowled at him, hurt.

"Jesus Christ," Thornton grouched, reaching for the bottle on his bedside table. "I said I was sor—"

He froze with his hand wrapped around the bottle's neck. He'd heard the sound again. It wasn't a hoof clomp or a horse's whinny, but a low, guttural growl swirling on the wind.

"There it is," he muttered, lifting his head and turning toward the window in the wall to the right of the bed.

"Damn!" he exclaimed when, as he twisted and stretched toward the window, a sudden pain seared the lingering, open sore in his right side. Holding his side with one hand, over the perpetually soggy bandage, he swung his legs to the floor, muttering, "Goddamn bitch!" and, placing his other hand on the bedside table, heaved himself to his feet.

"What?" Ruby said, cupping her breast and rubbing a thumb across the nipple, staring up at him now, curiosity tempering the injured look in her molasses black eyes.

The growl rose again, swirling slightly with the gusting wind.

"I thought you people were supposed to have such sharp senses," Thornton said, ducking his head to stare through the window, at the dust and leaves blowing this way and that about the yard. "You don't hear it?"

"The growling?"

"Yes, the growling!"

"I heard it," Ruby said, drawing the buffalo robe up to her neck and sinking deeper into the bed. "It's coyotes or wolves. They pick through the trash heap. So?"

"They pick through the trash heap, huh?" Thornton said, still staring out the window. "Or maybe they're in the barn — the door of which I see you left partway open when you went out to saw that quarter off the buck in there!"

Ruby drew the robe up around her jaws, regaining her injured expression. "I closed the doors!"

"Bullshit, you did!" Thornton turned to the girl, bending slightly at the waist, holding his side with one hand while pointing at the window with the other. "Suppose you tell me who opened it, then. The wind?"

"Maybe robbers opened it."

"Robbers!" Thornton laughed without mirth as he stepped into his elk-skin slippers and grabbed his revolver off the bedside table. "Hell, since the mine company moved the road, I'm so damn far off the beaten path, robbers don't even come around anymore!"

He opened the Colt's loading gate, spinning the cylinder to make sure all chambers showed brass, then grabbed the bottle off the table and threw back a long pull. The whiskey washed over his tongue, burning soothingly as it plunged down his throat and into his belly. It quelled the burn in his side but did nothing to temper his rage, which, while he'd waited these past several weeks for Temple to fetch his wayward, double-crossing whore, had been growling like a dry-summer lightning fire, consuming him.

He slammed the bottle down onto the table, causing Ruby to give a startled yelp, turning away from him. He shrugged into his tattered robe. Then, holding the pistol in one hand, the bottle in the other, he scuffed to the door, barking, "Gotta do every damn thing myself around here — is that the way it is? Jesus *Christ!*"

He went out and slammed the door to keep the heat in the room, as it was the only room he bothered to heat in these lean times, and stomped down the stairs. "Should have learned my lesson about hiring breeds after I hired that damn rock-worshipping heathen, Yakima Henry. Christ! There was a double-crossing son of a bitch!"

In the dark, dusty saloon hall, as ghostly silent as a catacombs, Thornton paused to sip from the whiskey bottle, then continued scuffing past the cold, bullet-shaped stove toward the front door. "Hired that son of a bitch, gave him a roof over his savage head and money in his buckskins, and how'd he repay me? By diddling and thus devaluing my best whore!"

Thornton pushed out the saloon's front door and, leaving the door open behind him, stepped out onto the front porch.

A chill blast assaulted him, blowing dust and leaves into his face. Cursing, he held his robe closed at his chest and, his thin hair sliding about his withered, sunken-cheeked head, dropped down the porch steps and headed across the yard.

As he approached the barn, gritting his teeth against the chill wind, Thornton raised his revolver, the growls, angry yips, and scuffs emanating from the barn growing louder with every step.

He sidled up to the partly open door and

shoved his head close to the gap, listening for a half second and then gritting his teeth furiously, thrusting the door wide, and bounding into the opening.

He stopped just inside the barn door and squinted into the musty shadows rife with the smell of fresh meat. He could hear the growls and snarls but could make out only a couple of jostling shadows until his eyes adjusted. Then he saw one of the coyotes literally hanging from the deer carcass that Thornton had bought a couple of days ago from a local mountain man, Wes Stanley. Stanley had hung the carcass from a ceiling to let it age.

The coyote's teeth were dug into a shoulder of the gutted buck. A shoulder was about all that remained, leaving only shredded, bloodred venison clinging to the comblike spine. Jerking its head back and forth and snarling, trying to free the shoulder from the socket, the coyote thrashed and kicked while another coyote was chomping part of the tailbone on the hay-strewn floor just below the scissoring, twisting hind feet of its zealous partner.

"Damn it!" Thornton bellowed, leveling the pistol and barking an echoing shot into the shadows.

The slug plunked into the carcass wetly.

The hanging coyote yipped with a start and dropped straight down to the floor.

"Steal my meat, will ya?" Thornton bellowed as he popped off another shot at the coyote dashing off into the barn's left rear shadows, its tail between its legs. Thornton drilled a shot at the other beast, blowing up dirt and straw a few inches in front of it.

The coyote yowled, darted away, then, unable to abandon its prize, bolted forward once more to snap up the bone between its jaws while eyeing Thornton defiantly.

Thornton fired again. Again the slug plowed into the floor as the coyote skipped and danced and dashed off into the barn's right rear shadows.

"Son of a bitch!"

He wheeled as the first coyote leaped over a hay mound to his left, angling toward the open door. Thornton fired at the blurred figure, but his slug crashed through a side window, and the coyote dashed on out the door flanking Thornton.

"Oh, no, you don't, ya damn scavenging savage!"

Thornton bolted out the door, his bathrobe dancing around his longhandle-clad legs, wincing sharply and clamping his hand to his aching side. He drew a bead at the coyote loping off down the trail east of the roadhouse yard, and triggered the Colt.

Dust and rocks blew up a good ten yards behind the fleeing beast, which swerved left from the trail and disappeared into the scattered aspens and pines.

Quick, rasping breaths sounded behind Thornton. He wheeled as the other coyote materialized from the barn's shadows, its gray-dun fur bloodied from its feeding frenzy, the three-foot length of the buck's tailbone clamped between its jaws.

Raising the revolver again, Thornton shouted, "No, you don't!"

As he triggered the Colt and heard the ping of the hammer slamming against the firing pin, empty, the coyote bumped the bone against the open barn door with a wooden thud.

Eyes wide above the bone in its teeth, its nostrils flaring as it breathed, the coyote turned sharply in front of Thornton and galloped westward past the mud-brick blacksmith shop and the windmill, angling toward the river meandering along the base of a high, stone cliff.

Thornton jogged after it, triggering the empty revolver and bellowing, *"Get back here, you mangy, thieving bastard!"*

His side grieving him, his chest rising and falling heavily, he tripped on a deadfall branch and dropped to his knees at a corner of the empty corral. He raked air in and out of his lungs, the cold air feeling like sandpaper, as he watched the coyote bound through the sage and scattered pines, leaping and swerving as though to mock the man he'd stolen good meat from, before disappearing into a ravine paralleling the stream.

"Son of a bitch!" Thornton rasped, his throat clenching, tears of rage rolling down his cheeks.

He cursed again, louder, and then again, even louder, until his throat gave out and he was only kneeling there, bawling, tears dribbling down his chin to splatter the sand and gravel beneath him.

"Stupid heathen," he grumbled after a time, grabbing a corral slat and pulling himself to his feet.

He turned toward the sprawling, weathered gray roadhouse, which looked gaunt and abandoned in the wind and flying leaves behind him, the paint chipping and peeling on the whipsawed pine boards, blown paper and tumbleweeds littering the porch. Plucking the whiskey bottle from his pocket and popping the cork, he stared at the window of the second-story room in which he'd left Ruby.

He tipped the bottle back, draining it, then tossed the bottle into the brush and pointed up at the window. "You left the damn door open, you stupid cow! The coyotes got the deer!"

Thornton stumbled forward, growling, snarling, and cursing. He crossed the broad yard, which was barren now, clean of all tracks save his own but which at one time had virtually always, day and night, teemed with saddle horses and freight wagons and roaring teamsters, drovers, and miners drunk on the beer and whiskey that Thornton had brewed in his storeroom.

Drunk, as well, on the whores — the best whores in northern Colorado/southern Wyoming — who had once entertained in all the upstairs rooms and who had scented the air with the soothing smells of perfume, incense, lilac water, and opium, and filled it with gay female laughter and the jubilant patter of piano music and singing.

"Goddamn her," Thornton snarled, stumbling up the rotting porch steps. "Goddamn her all to hell — runnin' off with that breed, makin' me look the fool. Forty years of bad luck caused by what?" He stomped through the open door, throwing his arms out for emphasis, fever sweat mixing with the tears streaming down his cavernous cheeks. "By a goddamn, double-crossing whore — that's what!"

"Bill? What was the shooting?"

The soft voice barely penetrated his consciousness. Midway through the dark saloon hall, he stopped suddenly and let his gaze crawl up the broad staircase.

Ruby stood at the top, holding a buffalo robe over her shoulders. Her feet were bare beneath the robe, toes curled against the place's penetrating chill. Her black hair hung straight down to her shoulders and her dark brows were furrowed warily.

Thornton's low-pitched voice rasped up from deep in his chest. "You left the barn door open. Coyotes got the meat."

"The wind must have blown it open," Ruby said weakly. "It catches it and slides it back."

"Goddamn heathen cow." Thornton reached into his pocket for the revolver, but stopped. The gun was empty. He looked around. The stove loomed to his left, flanked by a wood box. A few lengths of split stove wood lay inside.

Breathing heavily, his breath sounding like a rusty saw, he stumbled over to the box, picked up a length of split cordwood, and hefted it in his hand.

"Worthless bitch."

Ruby's eyes widened. "Bill, what are you going to do?"

"Gonna teach you what happens to double-crossing whores."

"Bill . . ."

Ruby let her voice trail off as Thornton kicked a chair out of his way and shambled toward the stairs, holding the wood down low in his right hand but staring up the staircase with savage menace in his eyes, his thin upper lip curled.

"Bill, no — it was the wind!" Ruby cried as she wheeled and ran off down the hall, bare feet slapping the musty auburn carpet runner.

Slowly, clenching the club tightly in his bony fist, Thornton climbed the stairs.

CHAPTER 21

Watching Yakima shot out of his saddle and then dragged by Wolf into the hills beyond the ranch had nearly stopped Faith's heart cold.

Seeing him fall from the passenger car's roof to roll off down the graded right-of-way, out of her reach once more, had been twice as jolting. She thought that her heart had really stopped beating for a couple of seconds, only to be shocked to life again by Lowry Temple grabbing a handful of her hair and pulling her straight back away from the window.

He'd jerked her around so brusquely, and tossed her back into her seat with such violence, that she'd nearly lost consciousness. Vaguely, she heard the outlaw leader laugh and announce, "Sorry you had to witness that little display, folks. But, ya understand, the woman's my *wife* and that *half-breed* ya saw in the window . . . well, let's just say their union wasn't sanctioned by the Lord, seein' as how they've made a mockery of our marriage vows!"

A few of the traveling women seated around Faith and Temple clucked their disapproval. A couple of the men gave their own opinions about how cheating women should be punished — especially women who cheated with savages — and Temple said, "Don't none of you worry. It looks like my cousins took care of the problem. I'm taking the little woman home to her pa, see if he can't do somethin' with her."

Faith looked up, her head and heart aching, fury kindling inside her once more, as Temple stared down at her, shaking his head with mock disapproval. "I figured I'd let the old man try to whip some sense into that pretty, whorin' ass of hers. I've done tried!"

One of the men — a drummer of some sort, judging by his cheap suit, pale skin, and derby hat — wished Temple luck as he castigated Faith with a look. Slumped in her seat, she stared straight ahead, reliving over and over the sight of Yakima's bloody face in the window, then his body tumbling down the hill below the tracks.

She bit her lip but could not hold back the sob bursting from her chest.

Temple, brushing soot and ashes from his

jacket and hat, stood across from her as Benny Freeze and Kooch Manley entered the coach door behind him, both looking windburned and exasperated. Manley held a hand to his scratched ear.

"You just go ahead and cry, woman," Temple said loudly enough for about half the car to hear over the roar of the iron wheels made louder by the sudden opening of the vestibule door. "Cry your eyes out over that heathen. Me, I've had it up to here with you!"

He sat back down in his seat across from Faith, furtive mockery in his gray eyes. Freeze and Manley sidestepped between him and Temple and sagged down in their seats, adjusting their holsters on their hips and looking around cautiously.

Manley, seated next to the window beside Temple and fishing a handkerchief from a pocket, leaned toward the outlaw leader and cast an accusatory glare at Faith as he said softly, "Chulo bought it, boss."

"I know, fool," Temple grumbled out the side of his mouth, staring straight ahead at Faith. "I saw . . . along with everyone else in the friggin' car!"

"He tried to fight that breed," Manley said, dabbing at his creased ear with the handkerchief. "The fool shoulda shot him, but you know how Chulo is."

"Was," corrected Benny Freeze, grinning to Faith's left. "I'm sorry Chulo's gone an' all. I mean, we was bonded partners." He hiked a shoulder and broadened his grin. "But I reckon with him gone, we can cut that bounty pie into bigger pieces. . . ."

Faith didn't hear the rest of the conversation. She curled up in her seat and turned inward, tending her grief, sorrow, and rage in a dreamy, brooding silence.

If Yakima was still alive after another violent encounter with her captors, it was unlikely he'd be able to sniff out her trail again. The man was as good a tracker as Faith had ever known — and she'd known many in her years as a working girl on the frontier — but he probably had no clue as to where Temple was taking her.

Besides, trains weren't all that regular in this neck of the frontier, and he'd be stranded out here without even a horse. . . .

She hadn't realized she'd fallen asleep until someone grabbed her coat and jerked her awake.

"Git up, you cheatin' bitch." Temple grinned down at her, his rifle scabbard in one hand, his saddlebags thrown over his other shoulder. "Time to switch trains."

Faith dropped her feet to the floor and

rose from her seat, only half feeling the aches in her sore, cramped muscles. Out the train windows, a thick, oily darkness — it must have been the middle of the night — was relieved by the fuzzy aura of bull's-eye lanterns and the crimson glow of cheroots and cigarettes.

She and the men disembarked from the train and moved with the crowd toward the brick station house on the brick-paved platform. A sign tacked to the depot announced BELEN, NEW MEXICO TERRITORY.

The wind howled — a bitter wind biting into her core. Smoke was torn to and fro across the frigid darkness.

As Faith moved like the undead, hollowed out by helplessness and grief, she gave little thought to beseeching assistance from the crowd.

As she approached the station house behind a pair of drummers in long wolf coats, mink hats, and leather grips, she saw an old man with a walrus mustache and a tin star pinned to his ratty buffalo coat. The constable leaned against a rain barrel, talking and laughing with a black porter while puffing a hand-rolled quirley.

As they approached the lawman, Temple squeezed Faith's arm warningly, but Faith had no intention of causing any more killings.

They waited out the ninety-minute layover in the depot house in which two potbellied stoves did battle with the bone-splintering, high-altitude cold. Then, when the Denver flier rolled in from the south, Temple ushered her onto the vestibule between a passenger car and a Pullman sleeper.

Temple turned left, opening a door of the sleeper car while pulling Faith along behind him.

"You got Pullman tickets?" Manley said, frowning incredulously at the outlaw leader while Benny Freeze moved up the steps behind him. Their breath puffed in the chill night air woven with unlit cinders.

"Me and the girl got the last compartment," Temple grunted around the cigar in his teeth. "Gonna keep her outta the crowd so we don't have any more embarrassing incidents."

As Manley and Breeze grumbled indignantly behind Faith, she let Temple pull her into the Pullman car in which all the compartments had been made up and a couple of kerosene lanterns smoked on the thinly paneled walls. Snores sawed through the sour, musty quiet as did a girl's soft chuckle.

Temple opened a compartment door,

jerked Faith in behind him. Nodding to a uniformed attendant passing along the hall, Temple closed the door and locked it.

He lit the single bracket lamp, then doffed his hat, hung it on a wall hook, and canted his head toward the double bunk beneath the window. Faith doffed her own hat and sagged back on the cot, the warmth from the charcoal brazier on the floor to her right feeling good against her legs.

She'd been so cold in the depot that the heat took her mind a little ways from her enervated fatigue. But when she looked up and saw Temple standing there in the half darkness against the door, running his hands through his hair and staring down at her darkly, she felt the old rage kindling inside her once more.

Her eyes dropped to the revolver jutting up from beneath his coat. Could she find a way to snatch it? She'd only get herself beaten or killed, and she'd never know what had happened to Yakima.

The outlaw chuckled. "Well, well — alone at last. Ain't this cozy, Mrs. Temple?"

"Diddle yourself."

"Got a sharp tongue on you." Temple sat down beside her on the double bunk. "My women don't speak to me that way. I don't allow it."

"I'm not your woman."

She gasped with a start as Temple pulled her toward him by her coat. He kissed her hard on the mouth, letting his lips linger over hers before he pulled back but continued clutching her coat in his fists. A devilish grin twisted his features, slitting his iron gray eyes. "Been wantin' to do that for a while."

Faith ran a sleeve across her mouth, revulsion churning in her gut. "I thought you didn't use force."

"That was just to see what's got that half-breed in such a goatish frenzy over you — riskin' life and limb to get you back."

Faith could feel the man's own goatish heat, see the lust in his eyes as he stared at her, the lewd grin frozen on his face. Suddenly, he drew her toward him once more and closed his mouth over hers.

She snapped her hands to his shoulders and began to push him away. She stopped, then flattened her palms against his shoulders. Though his rancid breath nearly made her wretch, she opened her mouth for him slightly, let him slip his tongue between her lips.

He pulled away slightly, his eyes meeting hers from two inches away — so close she could see the grime in the lines of his face, the tattoo in his forehead the color of old rifle bluing. "That's more like it."

He chuckled and kissed her again. Letting herself be kissed, she could feel the heat building in him as he mashed his mouth against hers, holding her painfully, his fingers gouging her back and arms. He slid one of his hands inside her coat and began unbuttoning her blouse, working hastily, grunting and sighing and wincing as he kissed her, his lust consuming him.

When he had her blouse unbuttoned, he shoved her away, grabbed the low neck of her camisole in both his fists, and tore it straight down the middle in one violent jerk. She leaned back against the curtained window, throwing her shoulders back, breasts out.

He knelt on the edge of the bunk, staring at her, his nostrils expanding and contracting, breath wheezing up from his throat.

As he moved toward her once more, his hungry eyes on her breasts, she sat up suddenly and flung her open right hand against his face.

The solid *smack* resounded about the small compartment.

Temple's head jerked with the force of the blow, his hair brushing down over his eyes. Rage burned in those dark orbs, replaced quickly with befuddlement.

"You can have me," Faith said just loudly enough to be heard above the car's slowly clacking wheels as they pulled away from the station. "But first I want your promise that you'll let me off the train at the first water stop."

Temple glowered at her, swaying and jerking slightly with the rock and pitch of the car. The bracket lamp cast shadows into the hollows of his cheeks, turned his eyes to coals on either side of the cross tattoo.

Faith held her breath, waiting.

If he gave his promise, he'd keep it. He was a man of honor, however dubious.

Unexpectedly, the outlaw leader's lips spread into a grin. He chuckled. The chuckle turned into a laugh, and he threw his head back on his shoulders, guffawing.

When his laughter had dwindled, he looked down at her once more and shook his head. "Once a whore, always a whore. Ain't that right?"

The words hit her like a clenched first. Frustration combined with anger made her tremble. Tears dribbled down her cheeks.

"Please," she begged, her voice quaking. "I'll do anything. . . ."

"Why?"

She stared at him, brushed tears from a

cheek with the back of her hand, and hardened her voice with bald disdain. "You could never understand, Temple."

He narrowed his puzzled eyes at her, cheeks flushing with fury, as though in a losing battle not only with her but with something in his own mind. "You're a fool. You could have any man you wanted. But you chose that half-breed, and now look where you're headed."

Shaking his head, he got down off the bunk and grabbed his hat off the wall hook. He snugged his hat on his head and opened the door to the sounds of snoring and the train's endless muffled roar. As he glanced back at Faith, she drew her blouse across her breasts and raised her knees to her chest.

"I'm goin' out for a smoke, but I'll be watchin' the door."

Temple stared at her, frowning as though trying to see inside her brain. Finally, he snorted caustically, shook his head, and dug around in his shirt pocket. He flipped a fifty-cent piece onto the bunk beside Faith.

"There you go — that's for the look. I've never cheated a whore in my life, and I ain't about to start now."

Temple winked, his eyes still bright with a confused, toxic mix of humiliation and barely contained fury, and went out, closing the door behind him.

Faith wrapped her arms around her legs, rested her head on her knees, and succumbed to her misery.

CHAPTER 22

Yakima waited until he was good and full of the Irish barman's chili before he tossed a fifty-cent piece onto the counter for the refills of both chili and whiskey.

" 'Bout time." Harms stood beside him, where he'd been standing tensely, glancing at the owl-eyed cardplayers flanking them as he sipped his whiskey and waited for Yakima to finish his meal. Ironically, the prospector said, "Are you sure you don't want some more?"

"Nah."

Yakima pinched his hat brim at the Irishman who stood off down the counter, scowling at him and Harms while rubbing a towel around the inside of a beer schooner. "The horses have had a fair blow. Let's get some grain and pull foot."

"There's an idea," Harms grumbled as he followed Yakima to the door, casting one more wary glance at the men behind him, all of whom stared back moodily over the pasteboards in their hands. "I'm tired of that big red target on my back."

As Yakima stepped out onto the porch, the cold wind blowing the fine, slanting snow in his face, boots thumped to his left. He turned to see a bearded, potbellied gent in a worn wool coat, vest, and pin-striped trousers approach the saloon door, scowling. A sheriff's star hammered from a peach tin glinted on his vest. His eyes were rheumy, his breath reeked of drink, and there was a smudge of women's face paint on his right cheek.

The sheriff sized up Yakima and Harms quickly, and licked his chapped lips, peeved at being called away, no doubt, from a whore's crib. "Someone said they heard shootin' over here. What's the trouble?"

"No trouble, Sheriff," Yakima said, continuing on past the man and descending the porch steps. "Just a little rule change is all."

Yakima grabbed Wolf's reins and the vinegar dun's halter rope from the hitch rail and began leading the horses at an angle across the broad main street in which the mudded wheel ruts had frozen and acquired a thicker snow dusting than before.

Snugging his hat down tight on his head, he headed for a large sign announcing GA-

BRIEL'S GRAIN. Harms followed, glancing over his shoulder to see the sheriff staring after him and Yakima, scowling as he fingered his thick gray beard.

The Easterner was certain that the sheriff, after finding out about the unseemly events in Lucky Joe's Saloon, would come calling on him and Yakima. But, to his pleasant surprise, he saw nothing of the sheriff again until after he and Yakima had bought a sack of oats, a couple of boxes of ammo, two pounds of jerky, and were mounted up and heading out of town into a light but chill, snow-spitting breeze.

Harms spotted the sheriff moving in the same direction they were on the street's left-side boardwalk.

As he and Yakima passed, the sheriff glanced toward them, eyes wary. The man paused, scrutinizing them with wary speculation. Choosing the doxies over a possible lead swap with strangers when he was probably making only twenty a month — and this cold was aggravating his rheumatism — he turned into a pink-curtained, plank-board shack and closed the door quickly behind him.

"Well, there's a good bit of luck."

Yakima glanced at Harms. "What's that?" His mind was on nothing now but the trail ahead, and his woman at the end of it.

"Nothing."

Yakima adjusted his holster on his thigh and spurred Wolf into a lope. "Let's ride!"

The half-breed winced as the wind lashed him, then raised the thick collar of his jaguar coat. He gave Wolf his head. The black mustang and the vinegar dun had perked up after the rest and the handful of oats he'd given them. Also, the cool air, hovering right around freezing, seemed to invigorate them, and they made good time for the rest of the day.

They stopped after dark in a small mining village — really just a large camp of tents and stone-and-log hovels, with goats and a couple of pigs running free. There, while they were watering their horses at the creek, a stout Italian widow sent one of her two shy, gangly boys out to invite them to supper.

They'd only stopped to rest the horses, boil some coffee, and chew some jerky, but Yakima and Harms gladly accepted the jovial woman's invitation.

As there were only four other families in the camp, isolated in the mountains just northeast of Taos, New Mexico, Yakima figured she was lonely for company. Finished with their small but hearty helpings of mountain goat stew, they were forced to parry the beseechings of the old widow, who insisted they stay till morning. They thanked her, left some coins on a stump outside the shack, and once more continued their northeastward journey between mountain ranges and known Indian camps.

Continuing to switch mounts every hour, they kept up a brutal pace. The snow turned to a light rain as they rode out of the mountains, and a couple hours later, the rain stopped and the stars appeared.

During a treacherous river crossing, Yakima nearly lost the vinegar dun when the horse started at a prospector's sluice box drifting past in the glittering black water. Not long after someone took a couple of shots at them — Yakima figured it was stockmen riding night herd and mistaking them for rustlers. He and Harms didn't return fire, but only kept their heads down and continued loping through the starlit night given voice every once in a while by owl hoots, coyote yips, and wolves howling from pine-studded scarps.

They gained the Santa Fe's north–south line when they spilled out of the mountains the next morning, just east of the rollicking mining camp of Colorado Springs.

It was a haggard, half-asleep pair that followed the tracks into Denver.

It was virtually a pair of corpses — wind- and sunburned, famished, and exhausted, their bones nearly literally disjointed by the long, hard, jarring pull — who didn't so much dismount as tumble out of their saddles at the stock corrals near Denver's bustling Union Station.

"Gotta question for ya." Harms sprawled over a top corral slat, his arms hanging down the other side and his cheek snugged up to the rail's weathered top. His glasses hung halfway down his nose.

Yakima tried to walk but dropped to his knees beside Wolf, the black stallion hanging its weary head and standing there, duck footed, dusty, and sweat silvered. One of the Indian ponies dropped and rolled, blowing hard.

"What's that?" Yakima said.

"In our conditions, how in the hell are we going to get Faith away from those killers?"

"That's a good question."

Wincing, Yakima dug his heels into the cinder paving beneath him and heaved himself to his feet, steadying himself with one hand on Wolf's back. He reached under the horse's belly to fumble the saddle cinch loose.

"I'll let you know when I got her figured.

Right now I'm gonna go on into the station, see when . . . if . . . their train got in."

"You do that," Harms said as Yakima began stumbling his way through the stockyards and warehouses, heading for the vast sandstone depot hulking up above the maze of corrals and bellowing cattle in the east. "I'll be right here when ya get back."

Harms dropped to his back and tipped his hat over his eyes.

Yakima was frustrated to learn at a ticket window in the marble-floored station that the last train from the south had pulled in four and a half hours ago.

That meant that Faith's kidnappers had no doubt acquired horses and continued their trek north toward Thornton's Roadhouse between then and now. If they'd decided to lay over in Denver until tomorrow, he had only a slight chance of finding them in this boisterous ranching and mining town of nearly thirty thousand souls, with nearly that many rail or stage travelers passing through at any given time.

He and Harms stabled their weary mounts in the first livery barn they ran into, then pondered their situations in a Chinese eatery across the alley, over roast beef sandwiches and thick, dark beer that the

Chinaman who ran the place hauled in wooden buckets from a nearby Irish saloon.

They didn't mull the situation long, half asleep and made sleepier by the food and beer, before they realized there wasn't much to ponder.

They and their horses were too trail beat to continue their trek until at least the next sunrise. All they could really do that night by way of trying to locate Faith was stumble around Denver's main thoroughfares, keeping an eye out for her kidnappers in the event they'd decided to lay over for some tavern crawling or whoremongering.

When, by nine o'clock that night, Yakima and Harms had had no luck finding Faith or any of the gang that had kidnapped her, they hunted down a room with a double bed, shared a couple of drinks from a bottle, rolled under the coarse wool blankets, and slept like dead men.

They were awakened at cockcrow by the indignant screaming of a drunk whore in the alley behind the little flophouse in which they'd rented a room, not far from their horses.

After a hasty breakfast in the same Chinese eatery in which they'd taken supper last night, they mounted up and headed west before the sun was up, the only traffic on the cobbled streets being that of milk and coal wagons, the only sounds that of roosting pigeons, sniffling paperboys, and the *snick-snicks* of the street sweepers' brooms.

Yakima had spent time in a Denver boardinghouse after his mother died, and he'd hauled freight around and prospected in the Front Range of the Rockies, so he knew this country. And having hauled freight for Thornton himself, he knew the shortest route between Denver and Thornton's Roadhouse northwest of Boulder and Camp Collins. He had no idea if Faith's captors knew the same route, but if he and Harms didn't overtake them on the trail, they might get there ahead of them.

Following old stage and Army trails, and even a few ancient Indian routes still visible beneath the prairie bromegrass and needle grass, they loped northwest into the shelving foothills. The sun touched Long's Peak and then, gradually, Bierstadt, the Twins Sisters, and the other lesser peaks standing around them.

Yakima was beaten and battered, and he ached in every muscle and bone. It had been a brutal couple of days. He rode wearily, but he rode hard, and Harms, who had no stake in this claim except friendship, did the same.

When he had Faith again, they'd head back to Arizona, and he'd harbor no more misgivings about their future. They'd rebuild the cabin as well as their remuda, and they'd continue selling horses to the Army outposts around the territory.

They'd savor each day they had together, and they'd let fate take care of the years. Because he loved her, and Harms was right. Love was rare.

The high crests quartered off to the south and east as he and Harms, angling northwest, left the rolling prairie and plunged into the rugged, pine- and aspen-studded mountains by way of one of many stream-carved canyons — one that Yakima knew was the shortest route to the canyon in which Thornton's lay.

Riding to Yakima's right, Harms cursed sharply through his teeth and lunged slightly forward in his saddle, grabbing his right thigh.

Yakima, holding the vinegar dun's reins taut in his left fist, turned to his partner, frowning. "What — ?"

He cut off the question himself when a rifle crack flatted out over the canyon around them, echoing sharply and sending magpies screaming from a cottonwood standing tall along the stream to Yakima's left.

He jerked his gaze up a rock- and juniper-studded ridge. Halfway up the ridge lay a slag pile from an abandoned mine, below the mine's coal black, wood-framed portal. Sluice boxes ran downslope from the portal toward the stream — weathered gray and grown up with weeds and shrubs.

On the slope above the slag pile, smoke puffed. There was a loud *thwhack!* and the Indian pony beneath Yakima screamed shrilly and leaped straight up in the air. As the rifle's report reached Yakima's ears, the vinegar dun landed on all four hooves before swaying sharply left, its legs seeming to melt beneath it.

Watching Brody Harms tumble off the back of his own pitching, whinnying Apache mustang, and knowing his dun was going down, Yakima released Wolf's lead line and threw himself forward over the dun's left wither.

He hit the slope on a shoulder and rolled as two more rifle reports cracked from atop the slag heap. When he stopped rolling and looked up, the mustang was on its side at the edge of the trail above, lifting its head, screaming, and thrashing its legs while blood pumped onto the dry brown grass around it. At the same time, the other three horses, including Wolf, galloped straight up the trail, buck-kicking and screaming.

From his angle, Yakima couldn't see Harms but he could hear the man groaning back up on the trail, on the other side of the wounded dun.

"Shit!" Yakima stared after the horses kicking up dust as they dwindled into the distance beyond a small miner's shack about fifty yards up the trail. Yakima's Winchester was in his saddle boot.

As more rifle cracks echoed around the canyon, the bullets plunking into the trail and slicing into the grass around Yakima, he grabbed his Colt. The ambushers were too far away for accurate shooting with a revolver, but he triggered two quick shots as he dug his heels into the grassy slope and bolted back up onto the trail.

Harms was lying beside the thrashing Apache pony, just out of reach of the dying horse's lunging hooves. Yakima drilled a bullet through the dun's head, ending its misery, and flung another slug toward the slag heap.

He dropped to a knee beside Harms.

The Easterner had taken a bullet in his right thigh, and blood, glistening crimson in the cool golden sunlight washing down between wintery mountain clouds, soaked his trouser leg above the knee.

Yakima winced as the shooters flung two more rounds into the trail around him. "How bad?"

Harms clutched his leg and stretched his lips back from his teeth. "I'd like to tell you it's just a scratch, but I'm afraid the bastards pinked me good."

CHAPTER 23

Yakima triggered another shot up toward the slag heap, then flung Harms's right arm around his shoulder and pulled the man to his feet. The Easterner balked, cursing.

Yakima adjusted the man's weight on his shoulder and lunged forward. "I'm gonna get you up to that shack yonder!"

Half dragging, half carrying Harms, Yakima sort of shuffle-jogged up the trail, staying to the right side where a cutbank capped with cedars and junipers partially concealed them from the shooters perched on the slag heap.

The half-breed's chest swelled anxiously.

If the men on the slag heap were Faith's captors, Faith was up there, as well.

Several more shots barked from up the slope, spitting gravel and cedar twigs onto the trail or ticking off Yakima's and Harms's hats. As they approached the cabin — door-less and windowless and missing shakes from its roof, its stovepipe rusted and dented — another shot from above plunked into a boulder flanking the place. Another careered off the roof, spraying splinters, before whining off over the canyon toward the stream.

Yakima gentled Harms down against the cabin's front wall, helping him stretch his legs out in front of him. Harms tipped his head back against the wall, sucking air through his teeth and squeezing his thigh with both hands.

"Leave Apache country only to get bushwacked by white men in Colorado," Harms growled. "My father was right — I'm a damn fool."

"Shut up." Yakima ripped off his green neckerchief and slipped it under his partner's bloody thigh. "I didn't expect them to know this trail — nor for us to catch up to 'em so fast. They must have lingered in Denver, and they know the country."

Harms was breathing heavily, sweat rippling down his ruddy cheeks, his body heat fogging his glasses. "If it's them, Faith's up there. How're you gonna get to her? It's three against one now." He added quickly with a wince, *"Goddamnit!"*

"Ain't sure. I've only heard one rifle so far." Yakima drew the bandanna taut around

Harms's thigh, just above the wound, and tied it. "I'm gonna fetch my Winchester, then go up and take a look, make sure it's not just owl hoots wantin' our horses."

He slipped his revolver from its holster, knocked out the spent shell casings, and thumbed fresh ones from his belt through the Colt's loading gate. "Keep that knot tight and don't move around much, or you'll bleed out. I'll be back soon."

"I reckon I'm not going anywhere," Harms rasped as Yakima peeked out around the corner of the cabin.

The shooter, who'd fired only one more shot since Yakima and Harms had taken cover, triggered his rifle again now, smoke puffing atop the slag heap. The slug barked into the side of the cabin with a sharp, echoing thump.

Yakima returned the bullet and bolted out from behind the cover, running up-trail in the direction the horses had fled.

He sprinted across thirty yards of open ground, the shooter squeezing off only one close round, blowing up dirt on the far side of the trail and behind Yakima, before the cutbank rose again to Yakima's right. He continued, keeping his head beneath the cutbank upon which the pines were now growing taller and thicker, giving good cover.

Finding Wolf standing owl eyed in a meadow horseshoeing out toward the stream sheathed in aspens, ash, and cottonwoods, he eased up to the jittery stallion, holding his hands out placatingly. The Apache horses were grazing about sixty yards west, in the shade of the trees near the edge of the water.

Behind Yakima, the rifleman was continuing to jack rounds into the cabin, the bullets sounding like flat hammer blows from this distance. The stallion flinched with every crack, peering behind, its black eyes wary.

"Thanks for runnin' out on me back there, you son of a bitch." Yakima slipped the Yellowboy from the saddle boot. " 'Preciate that." He was talking mostly to himself, distracting himself from his worry that the shooter or shooters, knowing he'd left his wounded partner behind, might be moving down the slope toward Harms.

Holding the rifle in one hand, he swung up onto Wolf's back and heeled the black into a lope back toward the main trail. He crossed the trail, rode a few yards back toward the cabin, then swerved sharply left, plunging up a narrow ravine lying perpendicular to the stream and rising up the gently sloping ridge.

When he'd ridden a good hundred yards, the ravine beginning to angle westward, away from the mine and the slag heap, Yakima dropped out of the saddle and left Wolf shaking his head and blowing angrily, ground-tied. The half-breed racked a shell into the Yellowboy's breech, pushed through a shadbush thicket, and climbed the side of a low ridge, following the intermittent rifle barks south and east.

A few minutes later, he climbed the slope flanking the slag heap, pulling himself up around mossy boulders, piñons, and junipers. Several yards down from the slope's crest, he stole along the hill's north shoulder until the mine portal opened above and to his right, on the east side of the rocky slope. The mine's black entrance looked like a gap between teeth, the rocks, gravel, and boulders of the slag heap slanting down beneath it.

Yakima stopped and looked around at the boulders and brush clumps, with junipers and potentilla growing out of the rocks and gravel. The shooting had stopped, and there was no sign of the shooter atop the slag heap before him, though several brass cartridge casings winked amongst the clay-colored rocks, where they'd been ejected from a rifle chamber.

Hair pricked along the back of his neck as he began moving forward across the slag, putting each moccasined foot down carefully. His heart thudded a warning that the bushwackers might have headed down to the cabin where he'd left Harms.

Suddenly, a chipmunk chattered raucously up the rocky slope on his right. Yakima dove forward as a rifle barked twice, the blue-red flashes showing against the black hole of the mine entrance. The slug cracked into the rocks off Yakima's heels, making his ears ring.

He came up off his shoulder and, from his knees, fired up the slope toward the mine portal — two quick bursts that echoed like cannon blasts around the canyon.

A man yelped. Yakima saw the figure staggering at the edge of the mine portal. There was a clatter as the man's rifle hit the ground. The man twisted sideways, dropped to his knees, and rolled down the slope toward Yakima.

The man piled up a few feet in front of Yakima's boots — a young, pale, sharp-faced hombre with a thin spade beard and a few tufts of untrimmed down on his cheeks. He wore a fur coat and green trousers. His hat had fallen off, and his thin light brown hair was sweat-matted to his head.

Yakima remembered his face from the cabin and then again from the train.

Blood seeped from two holes in the chest of his ratty fox coat. He arched his back and kicked, balling his cheeks with pain.

"Ya . . . ya half-breed bastard!" the kid spat, breathing hard as he writhed around on the rocks, blood pumping faster from the holes in his chest. "How many lives you got, anyway?"

Yakima looked around cautiously. The chipmunk berated him from a gray deadfall farther off down the slope, standing on its back feet and wringing its tiny hands. Deciding no one else was here, Yakima crouched over the dying younker and set his rifle across his thighs.

"One more than you do, kid. Where're the others?"

The kid cursed and groaned, kicking. Yakima held him still with the butt of his Winchester, and repeated his question.

"Gimme some water," the kid cried.

"Where're the others?"

The kid stretched his lips, his thin, mean face turning pale. "Went on to Thornton's."

He shaped a pained half smile as he ground his heels into the rocks. "Hell, they're probably almost there by now. For all these miles you come, you're gonna be too late to save that whore o' yours." He sucked another breath and stared mockingly up at Yakima. "Besides, she's Temples's whore now, anyways!"

Yakima stood, stepped back, and aimed the Yellowboy from his hip. Seeing the round, black maw yawning at him, the kid gained a horrified expression. *"No!"*

The call was clipped by the Winchester's bark. Yakima turned and walked away before the blood geysering from the kid's ruined forehead could splash his jeans.

"Admittedly, it don't look like much," said Lowry Temple as he trotted his rented bay around a long bend in the Thornton Canyon Trail, Bill Thornton having named the entire canyon in which his roadhouse sat after himself. "But it's home sweet home to you, anyway, my dear."

He glanced back at Faith, who rode a rented sorrel with one notched ear, her wrists and ankles once again tied to her saddle. As a giant fir pulled back off the trail's right side, the roadhouse slid out into the dusk-dim clearing before her — the sprawling, two-story affair that had, indeed, been home to her for nearly two years.

Her gut tightened at the sight. The place was a shadow of its former self — it looked abandoned and moldering from neglect, in fact — but the horror she'd endured here flashed in her mind, turning her blood to ice. Automatically, she turned a hopeful look behind her.

Lowry Temple, still watching her, shook his head. "That crazy breed of yours is a good ways back, probably still swapping lead with Benny."

"Shit," said Kooch Manley, riding his dun to Faith's right as they crossed the leaf-strewn yard toward the dark, ghostly road-house at the north edge of the clearing. "You think that kid's gonna clean his clock? Pretty clear to me that's one killin', determined breed, and that kid, crafty as he is, ain't no match."

"So?" Temple stared past Faith at the older gunman, Temple's stone-eyed face expressionless.

Manley laughed suddenly, as if getting a joke, their horses starting at a tumbleweed blowing across the yard before them. "I reckon I don't have nothin' against splittin' that seventy-five hundred dollars just two ways!" He slapped his thigh. "I reckon it's been a bit more adventurous journey than I throwed in for, and I reckon I'm due!"

As their horses drew to a halt before the roadhouse's dilapidated front porch littered with leaves and tumbleweeds, bromegrass growing up between the cracks, the older gunman looked at Temple suspiciously. "But I hope you ain't thinkin' you're gonna be eatin' the whole pie yourself now, partner."

The outlaw leader swung down from his saddle with a weary sigh. "Come on, Kooch. You know I ain't a greedy man." He glanced up at Faith sitting pale in her saddle, staring at the roadhouse's windows, some of which were boarded up or cracked, opaque with dust and grime. "But I do follow through on a job — don't I, honey?"

As Manley tended his own horse, Temple cut Faith's ankles free, then reached up to free her hands from the apple. "Let's go in and say hi to Mr. Thornton. He's gonna be right thrilled to see you."

She turned to him woodenly, her still features belying her thudding heart. "You don't need to do this, Temple."

"Why, sure I do. I made an agreement." Brusquely, Temple pulled Faith out of the saddle and set her down before him. "When a man agrees to something, he follows through."

"Otherwise, he can't expect to get no work elsewhere," Manley said, shucking his rifle from his saddle boot. "Ain't that right, Temple?"

"Quit your caterwaulin', Kooch. I wanna deliver this little trollop and get the hell outta here." Temple grabbed a handful of Faith's hair and pulled her head back painfully, running a gloved thumb across her smooth, pale neck. He gritted his teeth as he gazed into her face. "Can't say as I'm gonna regret comin' to the end of this trail. It most definitely is the *final* end for you, *honey!*"

Faith gritted her own teeth against the man's firm grip on her hair. "Why don't you stop your caterwaulin' and get on with it, then, Temple?"

Temple chuckled, grabbed her arm, and shoved her toward the porch. As Faith stumbled forward, she cast another glance back along the trail.

Yakima had come after her. Somehow, he'd followed. But the odds were stacked against them both, she realized now, as dread filled her belly like hot, rancid soup.

Somehow, she'd always known they were. The short life they'd lived in Arizona had been a dream.

Even if Yakima survived the latest ambush Temple had sprung on him, he'd be too late to save her. A luckless life was luckless to the end, and it put a hex on all who became entangled in it. Faith's past, wearing the mask of Bill Thornton, was about to finish her.

She moved up the porch steps behind Manley, Temple falling into step a safe distance behind her. He didn't have to worry, she thought. She was ready to end the charade. Her life had really ended here, after all.

One thing was for sure, though. Thornton would join her on the road to where all condemned souls journeyed.

Manley pushed through the door and stepped between the tied-back batwings. "Thornton?" the bounty hunter called, his voice echoing around him.

Faith moved in behind him, and her breath caught at the tawdriness of the place. The inside was as bad as the outside. At one time, Thornton's had been one of the best-kept establishments in the northern Front Range, with miners, freighters, and drovers riding from a hundred miles away to partake of the luxurious furnishings, fine liquor and beer, and gifted doxies.

Now the place was dark as a cave. Its musty air was rife with the smell of putrefying flesh and mouse droppings. Dust streaked the floor and tables and the long, mahogany bar running along the room's broad right wall. Bullet holes remained in the walls, ceiling, and bar from the night when Yakima had shot his way out of the place, after saving Faith from the four men who'd trapped her in her room with knives.

"Thornton!" Temple called toward the stairs at the broad saloon hall's far end. "It's Temple! We got your girl!"

Silence. The wind howled outside, blown dust ticking against the walls and windows. Then the ceiling creaked, as though someone were fumbling around in one of the rooms above the bar.

Temple turned to Manley. "Stay down here, Kooch. Keep an eye on the front." He grabbed Faith's left arm, squeezing hard. "I'll go up and deliver the package."

"I still say it's a damn shame you haven't let us partake of them goods," Manley said behind Temple and Faith, his words shattering the sepulchral silence. Faith could feel the man's heated gaze on her. "A girl built like that was put here for a reason."

Wincing against Temple's firm grip on her arm, Faith climbed the carpeted stairs. Revisiting this place, she thought, looking around at the dusty paintings, tintypes, and bracket lamps on the papered walls, was like revisiting a world she'd dreamed in another life. She had to remind herself it was real.

The place looked not only shabbier, but smaller. And it wasn't only the dust, the darkness, the peeling wallpaper, and the smell of sickness that made it look grim. It was her memories of the place. Memories from a time when this had been what she'd settled for.

Moving down the second-story hall, Temple's spurs trilling softly behind her, she saw a long oval shape on the floor in front of her, lying against the base of the left wall. Frowning, she approached the figure slowly, and gasped.

A person lying there. An Indian girl. She lay in a twisted, naked pile, her head resting on her left arm, which was flung out behind her on the sour-smelling runner. Her glassy brown eyes stared at the ceiling over Faith's shoulder. Her right knee was bent modestly over her other leg.

Her brown skin was a mass of bruises and blood-crusted cuts. Her cheeks and lips were smashed, and congealed blood had pooled thickly beneath her head. The whites of her eyes were a dark, grisly red.

Behind and above Faith, Temple chuckled. "Thornton must be practicin' up." He reached down and jerked Faith to her feet. "Come on, whore."

Faith stumbled off down the hall, Temple yelling behind her, "Thornton — you here? Brought the Christmas goose, Thornton!" Temple laughed. "She's primed for pluckin'!"

A muffled cough sounded. Thornton's unmistakable voice rattled, "In here!"

Temple grabbed Faith's arm, jerked her up before Thornton's office door on the right side of the hall. The wood plaque on the door, which she remembered well, read OFFICE. KNOCK FIRST!

Temple grinned at Faith and, leaning in front of her, turned the doorknob without knocking. He shoved the door inward. "Home again, home again, jiggidy-jig!"

CHAPTER 24

Temple shoved Faith into the office.

She lurched forward, snarling her indignance at the needlessly brusque firebrand, and stopped. Her mouth opened suddenly, lines spoking her eyes, but she managed to stifle the gasp that had started deep in her throat, when her eyes had settled on the cadaver sitting before Bill Thornton's massive, scarred desk fronting a curtained window in the opposite wall.

But it wasn't a cadaver sitting there, leaning back in Thornton's brocade swivel chair. No. Arms crossed on his concave chest, spindly legs raised, slippered feet crossed on the desktop, it was Thornton himself. The roadhouse manager wore a tattered, faded red and white plaid robe — one that Faith remembered — and longhandle underwear begrimed with many stains and spotted with cigar burns.

But what captured the brunt of Faith's attention was the man's bulbous head — the skin of his face drawn paper white between his cheekbones and his jaw, the hollows so deep that she could see his jaw hinges. His eyes were sunken deep in overlarge sockets. His hair, which she'd remembered as thin and light brown, was now little more than a few insubstantial strands nearly as pasty gray as his face.

His long neck seemed to be constructed solely of sinew amongst which his Adam's apple hung like a large gray spider caught in the web of some giant fly.

Thornton stared at Faith dully, the rheumy gaze registering only faint recognition. As he kept his eyes on her, his thin pink lips opened, and he puffed a fat cigar for a time before barking through a thick cloud of wafting smoke, "Leave us, Temple."

"Ain't you forgetting something?"

Thornton's voice was raspy and higher than she remembered. "Your money's downstairs at the bottom of the wood box. Help yourself to hooch, but there ain't much for food."

"We'll get by. We ain't stayin' long, anyways." Temple glanced at Faith as he turned slowly, haltingly to the door. He stopped, glanced back at Thornton. "You sure you can handle this polecat? I think she outweighs you, Thornton."

"Leave us!" Thornton barked, louder.

"All right, all right." Temple ran his appreciative gaze over Faith once more. Though he was grinning, he seemed reluctant to leave. Finally, he nodded at her briefly, pulled his gaze away, sauntered out the door, and drew it closed behind him.

Faith stared across the room at the little, gray-headed scarecrow leaning back behind his desk. Thornton met her gaze, holding it pensively as he puffed the cigar. Behind him, the light was fading, which seemed to intensify the light from the green and mauve Tiffany lamp on the desk to his right. The light burnished the smoke cloud billowing around his head.

Behind the rich smell of the tobacco and the coal-oil lamp lay the cloying odor of rotting flesh.

Thornton's chest rose suddenly. "How you been, Faith?"

She stood still as wax, her face expressionless. "Do what you're gonna do, you pathetic bastard. And get it over with."

Thornton smiled a death's-head smile as he rolled the wet tip of his cigar around on his lower lip. He canted his head sideways, as if indicating someone else in the room. "Did the boys have their way with you?"

Faith laughed suddenly, loudly at the irony. The possibility of her having been sullied by her captors was no doubt of far more interest to Thornton, a common roadhouse pimp, than it was to Yakima, her own man.

"No," she said, feeling her jaws tense as her eyes burned a hole through the devil before her. "I enjoyed *them*" — she smiled wickedly — "every chance I *got.*"

Thornton's lips stretched across his face like a knife slash, and he tipped his head back on his shoulders, guffawing. The laughter dwindled into rattling coughs, and he looked at Faith again through the smoke, his eyes wet. "I always loved your salty sense of humor. Such language seemed so out of place on such a pretty mouth. It's downright — what is it? Erotic."

Thornton gestured toward the orange-cushioned settee against the wall to Faith's right. "Why don't you take off your coat and sit down, so we can catch up?"

"Diddle yourself, you son of a bitch. You killed my brother and burned our cabin — Yakima's and mine. You ruined our lives. I've got no 'catching up' to do with you."

She moved forward, balling her fists at her sides, her blue eyes flashing like bits of polished glass. "I'm not gonna sit down so you can groom me for the killin' — try to put me at ease so the sudden knife slash will be all that more of a surprise. I gut-shot you and ran out on you, and you've obviously been stewin' over it for the past two years." She shook her head. "Well, your stewin's about to be over. Get up and face me like a man, you pathetic son of a bitch!"

Thornton's face had become a blank death mask once more, void of expression. Suddenly, he leaned back, opened the top desk drawer, and hauled out a silver-plated .38-caliber Smith & Wesson revolver — the one he'd always kept in his desk to deal with customers who'd tried to skin out on their bill, or double-crossing business partners such as freighters who'd tried to charge him too much for a whiskey haul.

For wayward whores he usually reserved his obsidian-handled, seven-inch stiletto. Two quick horizontal slashes across the lips, to brand them and ruin them for the only trade they had. Reducing them to animals so that, thrown back into the wild to which they were no longer accustomed, they'd soon starve or fall victim to the elements.

It was the S&W he clutched now, pointing the barrel at Faith as he heaved himself up out of the chair, red faced and sweating and reeking like a dead animal. As he moved out from behind the desk, he clutched his right side, just above his waist, wincing as though every movement pained him. His robe winged open slightly, and Faith saw a bloody bandage.

"Christ," she said, awestruck as she slid her eyes up from Thornton's side to his oily face growing before her.

"Yeah, Christ!" The roadhouse manager leaned down to snatch up a piece of split, stove-length wood that had been leaning against his desk. "That's your doin', bitch!"

Faith couldn't conceal her surprise. "That's where I shot you?"

Thornton straightened and continued moving toward her, the pistol in his right hand, the wood in his left. The wood was splattered with dried dark red blood. He spat his words out like phlegm-laced marbles, slitting his bulging eyes.

"Must've been a poisoned bullet you shot me with. What are you — a witch?"

Faith said nothing. She found herself backing toward the door.

She thought she'd prepared herself for the worst, but there'd been no way she could have prepared herself for the demonic ogre stumbling toward her now, wielding a pistol in one hand, a chunk of bloodstained wood in the other. His death smell made her eyes water.

It was the smell of a cave in which a wild beast had curled up and died.

Horror and revulsion nearly unhinged her. Stumbling backward, she backed into the wall. Thornton moved toward her, blowing his sour breath and raising the revolver, narrowing one eye as he cocked the hammer with a raspy click.

"The half-breed dead, is he?"

"Maybe." Faith stared at the gun muzzle yawning before her, and her resignation returned. She shaped an icy smile as she tipped her chin toward the window. "Maybe he's right out there."

"Follow you, did he?" Thornton slitted a rheumy eye and nodded. "Once a whoremonger, always a whoremonger."

"You should know, Bill."

Pressing the revolver to her forehead, he dropped the wood and reached toward her with his left hand, grabbed the collar of her coat, and jerked down. "Get out of them duds, whore! I'm gonna beat you naked!"

Thornton had more strength than he appeared to have. The coat's first two buttons gave, and Faith stumbled forward, knees bending. "No!"

"Out of them duds!" Thornton ordered again, giving the coat another tug while aiming the gun at Faith's head.

Buttons clattered to the floor and rolled while Faith, falling to her knees, tried to hold the coat closed against her chest. The coat opened, and as Thornton laughed mirthlessly and grabbed her shirt, Faith bounded up off her heels.

She nudged his gun aside and rammed her left fist, knuckles first, into Thornton's right side. She could feel the soggy blood and pus and the bandage padding the wound before she withdrew her fist and glanced at Thornton.

The eyes seem to pop out of the roadhouse manager's head, and, his face turning a shader pale of gray, he threw his head back on his shoulders and yelled like a trapped grizzly. Stumbling back and falling to one knee, he dropped the revolver and kicked it.

The gun spun past Faith toward the settee to her right.

"Ach! Goddamn . . . son of a bitch!" Thornton raged as Faith dove for the gun.

She hit the floor on her shoulder and slid across the puncheons, piling up against the settee and closing her hands over the gun. On one knee, Thornton turned toward her, his face a mask of pain and fury.

"Bitch!"

Thornton looked down, saw the blood-stained log. He grabbed it in his right hand

and pushed back to his feet. Wanting a good shot at the man, Faith gained her knees, then raised the revolver in both hands. He bolted toward her, faster than she'd thought possible. She'd just got the hammer cocked back before he was three feet away from her, swinging the log from back behind his shoulder, lips stretched back from his yellow teeth and purple gums.

Squinting one eye and holding her ground, Faith drew a bead on Thornton's forehead. Thornton was swinging the club forward when Faith squeezed the trigger.

The hammer pinged on a spent chamber.

Shocked, Faith glanced at the gun. Seeing the wood slamming toward her, she ducked slightly, turning sideways. It wasn't enough of a move to avoid the blow altogether, and a corner of the sharp-edged log caught her right temple with a resolute smack, dimming her vision and making her ears ring as she rose off her feet and flew sideways to pile up hard at the base of Thornton's desk.

Thornton threw his head back and shouted hoarsely toward the wainscoted ceiling, "Evil, wicked, double-crossing *bitch!*"

As he moved toward her, wobbling and stumbling over his own slippered feet, Faith, lying against the desk, blinked to clear her blurred vision. She brushed the back of her right hand against her left temple. The knuckles came away coated in blood.

Behind a strange tingling, she felt a throbbing inside her temple, just above her ringing right ear.

Heavily, still trying to clear her eyes, Faith scrambled to her feet. Thornton hauled the club back again for another blow. Faith threw her left arm up in front of her head. The club slammed into it, lifting her up off the floor and throwing her onto the desk.

She screamed as she rolled across the desk, sweeping a pen holder, ashtray, books, and the Tiffany lamp onto the floor with raucous clattering thumps and the scream of breaking glass. As she flew over the swivel chair and hit the floor behind it, grunting loudly as the air was hammered from her lungs, she heard a fiery whoosh and smelled the sharp, piney smell of coal oil.

In the periphery of her vision, she saw flames dancing up the curtains behind her. Both her ears were ringing now and she felt a tingling in her limbs. Rage and terror took over, and she scrambled back to her feet, feeling the heat from the flames pushing against her.

As the flames coiled up the curtains and the wall behind the desk, lighting the room bizarrely and sending smoke tendrils angling toward the ceiling, Faith bounded out from behind the desk. Thornton stepped between her and the door, blood showing thickly on his robe and stretching across his pot belly.

"Where do you think you're going?"

He swung the log. Faith ducked. The log sang through the air over her head.

Twisting around, she slammed her right elbow into Thornton's right side, evoking another thundering howl, and, using both hands and moving quickly, wrenched the log free of his grasp. She swung around toward Thornton, arms stretched out in front of her, both hands on the log.

The end of the log caught Thornton low on his left cheek and carved a long, deep gash across his lips. Thornton's head flew sideways.

"Butcher!" Faith cried.

Shifting her weight from one foot to the other, she swung the log back in the opposite direction, and it caught Thornton straight across the mouth. Lips bursting like a ripe tomato, Thornton's head jerked up, and he gave a muffled, exasperated "Hng-hah!" as he stumbled back, hands flailing toward the desk edge.

Holding the edge of the desk with one hand, he teetered slowly sideways toward the floor, his eyes fluttering.

Feeling blood dribble down the side of her head, Faith moved toward him, raising the club once more with both hands. She gritted her teeth and savored the sight of the man — bloody faced and horror-struck — staring back at her beseechingly.

Only his eyes begged for mercy. His jaws slid around brokenly.

"I'm no witch," Faith snarled, her own voice reaching her ears as if from far away, the roadhouse manager's image shifting this way and that before her. "All your bad luck you brought on yourself, you simple son of a bitch!"

With that, she raised the log above her head.

Thornton's eyes grew wide as he silently begged for mercy. His mouth opened but only blood spewed across his lips.

Faith smashed the log down across his skull with a resolute thud. Thornton fell heavily to the floor at the base of the desk — screamless, his slender legs spasming and his broken jaws clattering as they opened and closed of their own accord.

Faith grabbed her pounding head and glanced around. The flames had spread to three walls and were snaking across the ceiling toward the wall bordering the hall.

Smoke hung thick as dirty cotton, stinging her eyes and nostrils.

She turned away from Thornton's still-spasming body and began moving toward the door. She made it only halfway before her eyes went dark, her knees turned to putty, and she dropped with a gasp.

CHAPTER 25

Yakima smelled the smoke on the cold wind.

Galloping west along the trail cleaving Thornton's Canyon, he glanced back at Brody Harms hunched atop his mustang. Since it was twilight, the half-breed couldn't see much but the last light reflected in Harms's glasses and his exposed white teeth as he leaned forward with a pained grimace to clutch his wounded thigh.

"I'm gonna race on ahead!"

"I'll be right behind you!" Harms shouted, his voice taut with resolve.

Yakima heeled Wolf into a ground-eating gallop, firs and pines passing in a blur along both sides of the trail, the silver-glinting stream rushing over rocks and deadfall logs to his left. He passed an abandoned prospector's cabin grown up with shrubs, and braced himself as he traced what he recognized as the last, long curve in the trail before the clearing in which Thornton's

Roadhouse sat.

An anxious scowl bit into his forehead as he peered skyward, the low, dark clouds touched with flickering umber and tendrils of white smoke. Hunched low in the saddle, he and Wolf raced around the last dogleg in the trail, bringing the clearing up in front of them.

Thornton's sat to the right, flames licking out a second-story window with white smoke pouring out around them. The flames were leaping up above the window to the roof and down the wall toward the porch below it. Wan light lit the first-story windows, including the large one left of the door and under the porch's sloping, shake-shingled roof.

Yakima's chest tightened and his gut rolled as he turned the horse to the roadhouse. Wolf was still lunging forward when Yakima leaped out of the saddle, lost his footing, fell, and rolled.

He came up pulling his .44 out from beneath his coat and running in long strides toward the roadhouse, the dragon's breath of the flames wheezing and roaring above his head.

He could hear men shouting inside as he leaped up the porch steps in a single bound. Thumbing his Colt's hammer back, he tripped the front door's latch perfectly as he smashed his shoulder against the door panel. The door flew open, slamming back against the wall, and just over the threshold, Yakima dropped to his knee and raked his eyes around the dim room into which the smoke from upstairs was seeping.

"Hey!" a man shouted in surprise — a shadowy figure wheeling toward Yakima from near the large, bullet-shaped wood-stove.

Cold steel flashed low on the man's silhouette, and Yakima's Colt barked and leaped in his hand. The man screamed and stumbled backward, twisting sideways, his own revolver exploding into the ceiling. Another figure at the top of the stairs, wheeling toward Yakima, angled a rifle down the stairs.

The rifle flashed and cracked. The slug barked into the puncheons three feet in front of Yakima. Yakima rolled as another explosion followed the rasp of a cocking lever. The second slug tore into the floor to Yakima's left.

Yakima rolled onto his belly, angling his Colt straight out from his chest and aiming up the stairs.

Pow! Pow! Pow!

The .44's explosions echoed around the

saloon hall. At the top of the stairs, the man with the rifle grunted. There was a smashing clatter as the rifle hit the floor and the man rolled down the stairs, cursing.

His voice trailed off as he followed his still-rolling rifle down the stairs. He was still rolling when Yakima scrambled back to his feet and bolted forward, yelling, "Faith!"

The dead rifleman hit the floor at the bottom of the stairs. Yakima leaped over the man's bulky body, gaining the stairs on the third step and taking the rest three at a time, holding his cocked revolver out before him.

He turned at the top and ran down the hall, yelling for Faith and squinting against the smoke and flames seeping around a closed door halfway down the hall. Turning the doorknob quickly, he pushed the door open.

The blast of fresh air from the hall made the burning walls and ceiling inside the room growl like a suddenly aroused lion, instantly gaining intensity. The searing heat pushed against Yakima, soaking his shirt with sweat.

"Faith?"

Crouching, he darted into the room. Two figures lay on the floor — one belly-down, blond hair fanned across her head. Thornton lay beyond Faith. The roadhouse manager was on his side, mouth half open as though in midspeech, his death-glazed eyes orange with leaping flames.

Yakima dropped to a knee over Faith and touched her shoulders. She jerked with a start and a muffled gasp.

"It's Yakima." Gently, he turned her over, winced at the blood streaming down from her right temple. "I'm gonna get you out of here."

Yakima snaked one arm under her neck, the other under her knees, and rose. Tears and sweat from the heat and smoke streamed down his face as he hurried to the hall door. He started out, stopped, and turned back into the room, where Thornton lay seemingly staring at him with glassy, orange eyes.

"Burn in hell, bastard."

With Faith in his arms, Yakima turned and went out, striding quickly down the smoke-filled hall, then down the stairs, holding Faith secure in his arms. She groaned and turned her head and tried lifting a hand to his face.

"Easy," Yakima said as he gained the bottom of the stairs.

He stepped over the dead rifleman and, glancing at the tattoo-faced man lying prone near the stove, continued across the saloon hall, out the front door, and onto the porch. He eased down the steps and walked into the hard-packed yard lit by the growing fire in the roadhouse's second story.

He gently eased Faith onto the ground and leaned over her. His face only inches from hers, he slid her hair back from her cheeks. "Faith. Can you hear me?"

She groaned and coughed as her chest spasmed. Her eyes opened partway. They had a confused, faraway look before they finally focused on Yakima. The corners of her mouth rose, and her gaze softened.

"I'm sorry," she said. "I should have bought us more time."

Yakima shook his head and kissed her cheek. "You don't have anything to be sorry about. We have plenty of time. I'll get you back to Denver, look up a sawbones."

She placed a finger against his lips. "I love you, Yakima. I always would have."

"We'll go back to Arizona, rebuild the cabin."

She smiled up at him. Tears shone in her eyes.

"Thornton's dead. You got him." Yakima slid his hands under her once more. "I'm gonna get you on a horse, and . . ."

As he began to rise from his knees with Faith in his arms, her head wobbled to one side. Her eyes fluttered and turned glassy. Yakima stared down at her, his tongue dry, his mouth open as if to speak but not saying anything until finally her name brushed over his lips like the rustling of a parched, inner breeze.

She lay slack and silent, her head tipped slightly to one side as though staring up at the room in which Yakima had found her.

He shook her slightly. "Faith?"

Her head wobbled and her arms, hanging slack, jostled, her fingertips brushing the ground, her boot heels making a soft scraping sound in the dirt.

Yakima knelt stone-faced with shock, staring down at Faith lying still in his arms.

Vaguely, as though the sounds came from another plane, he heard a man shout, "Breed!" Boots thumped above the roar of the flames spreading down from the second-story window to the porch roof.

Another voice that he absently registered as that of Brody Harms cried, "Yakima, look out!"

There was the crackle of gunfire behind him and ahead. Yakima did not respond to the shots. He continued staring down at Faith, his heart thudding dully.

Boots thumped and spurs rang like cracked bells.

Again, guns flashed in the night. A man groaned. Yakima turned slowly to see a figure stumble down the porch steps and fall facedown in the yard.

The man's head rose from the ground, the cross tattooed into his forehead seeming to pulse and glow, and then there was another gun flash and bark.

The man's head dropped like a stone.

Yakima turned back to his woman.

"Faith?" He supported her head with his knee and one hand while smoothing her hair back from her temple with the other.

Scuffing sounds rose as Brody Harms, holding his smoking revolver down low in his right hand, ambled toward Yakima, dragging his wounded right leg. The man dropped to a knee. His broad chest rose and fell sharply as he breathed. He said nothing.

Yakima looked at him. The fire danced in the Easterner's dusty spectacles, but they could not conceal the lines of horror etched like spokes around his eyes. He reached out to lay a finger to Faith's neck. After a moment, he raised his stricken eyes to Yakima.

He dropped his gaze and removed his glasses.

The half-breed looked down at his woman sagging in his arms, and shook her one more time. Her eyes continued staring at the leaping flames, sightless, tear-glazed. On her lips was etched a fateful, beguiling half smile.

Yakima threw his head back on his shoulders. His cry careened across the night and echoed toward the stars.

"Faith!"